The F Factor

Best Wishes

Lorraine Hopkins.

The F Factor
forty, footloose & frisky

Lorraine Hopkins

STELLAR★BOOKS

Published in 2017 by:

Stellar Books
1 Birchdale
St Mary's Road
Bowdon
Cheshire
WA14 2PW
UK.

E: info@stellarbooks.co.uk
W: www.stellarbooks.co.uk
T: 0161 928 8273
Tw: @stellarbooksllp

ISBN: 978-1-910275-191

Copyright © Lorraine Hopkins 2017

A copy of this book is available in the British Library.

An eBook of this publication is available from amazon.co.uk

Typeset in Banda Regular and Garamond.

Cover by: Jane Dodds. E: janebdodds@ntlworld.com

The author has asserted her right under the Copyright, Designs and Patents Act 1988 to be identified as the author of this work.

All rights reserved. No part of this publication may be altered, reproduced, stored in a retrieval system or transmitted in any form or by any means, electronic, mechanical, photocopying, recording or otherwise, except as permitted by the UK Copyright, Designs and Patents Act 1988 without the prior express permission of the author.

The most inspirational people are those who are always there for you.

For Bev, with love.
XX

Table of Contents

Acknowledgements viii

1 First Things First... 1
2 Bin Here Long? 7
3 Cross County and Cross Trainers 15
4 Good Vibrations 25
5 Next Stop the Olympics! 31
6 In Retail Therapy 42
7 Virgin on the Ridiculous 51
8 Fuzzy Navels and Fuzzy Heads 61
9 Plethora of Pillocks 66
10 Nudge Nudge, Wink Wink! 79
11 G'day Sheila … or is it Bruce? 89
12 It's Big, it's Hairy and it's Bloody Scary! 109
13 Ssshunssshine in Paradise 118
14 Sea Legs and Sea Creatures 126
15 Tears and Tribulations 138
16 The Waiting and Dating Game 144
17 Orville CAN Fly!! 157
18 F Bomb to Sex Bomb 172
19 Bunk Beds, Fleeces and Ear Plugs 189
20 The Key to a Good Relationship… 209

21 Home Invasion of the Creepy Kind.................. 218
22 Through the Keyhole 229
23 New Pad and New Beginning 241

About the Author 251

Acknowledgements

'You should write a book.' How many times had friends and family said that to me after being entertained by my latest faux pas? So, after lots of encouragement, and an odd glass of wine, that's what I decided to do.

All the characters in the book are fictional, but some of the predicaments Isobel finds herself in are based around real events in my life.

This book is dedicated to those of us who have a knack of saying, or doing, the stupidest of things at the most inappropriate moment: if nothing else it provides the material for a good story.

The book evolved from being a pastime that I thoroughly enjoyed and could throw myself into, to being a reality. For this I'd like to thank my publisher and proof reader, whose editorial polishing skills are on a par with Mr Sheen. Without her help, I wouldn't have enjoyed the journey from manuscript to print half as much.

I'm also fortunate to have very supportive family and friends, who have been there for me through my entire life. I could not have written this book without you, not just for some of the material, but for also giving me the courage to try. You're my rocks to cling to, my drinking buddies to embarrass myself with, and you bring me love and joy in equal measures.

All my love always

Lorraine

1

First Things First....

A new start and a new life. That was my mantra.

Let me introduce myself: I'm Isobel Parkes. I'm a single 46-year-old, with a love for life and an uncanny knack of getting myself into all sorts of situations. Mayhem and chaos seem to be my new best friends, especially since swapping the stability of couple cosiness for the unfamiliar world of single insanity. Although my marriage of 20 years had been a happy one, I felt we had drifted. What was life for if not for living?

Unfortunately, this brave decision also coincided with the hitting of hormonal hell, which is aptly named the fuzzy years; an endearing term for a time in your life when everything goes to pot. My brain disintegrated into a pile of mush, my libido hit an all-time high and my emotions became more unstable than a chair with two legs. A woman as horny as hell with the thinking capacity of a stunned sheep is not a great combination.

So, it was with great trepidation that I moved out of the family home with my barmy cocker spaniel,

Ferdinand. Yes, I know what you're thinking, that's an odd name for a dog. What you need to appreciate is that my family are all Manchester United fans and so when naming the dog, it was a choice between that or Nani. I somehow had visions of people thinking I was looking for an eccentric elderly relative on the field if I was heard shouting, 'Nani. Will you come out of that bush?'

Naming your dog can be quite important; I remember meeting an elderly gentleman searching for his dog. He was stood there by these large shrubs with an empty lead shouting,

'Cedric. Cedric. Come on boy, where are you?' Me, being the helpful person that I am, decided to see if I could help in any way.

'Is your dog lost?' I asked. 'Oh yes, dear. Could you help? My little Cedric went into that bush about ten minutes ago. He won't come out and I can't get to him. I've tried biscuits and everything.'

Now at this point most people may ask what sort of dog it was, but there stood this frail elderly gentleman so I assumed that it was a small terrier maybe, especially with a name like Cedric. Lesson one: never make assumptions.

I crawled on my hands and knees, armed with a biscuit, under this prickly bush while the man held on to my dog.

'Cedric! Come on, boy..' I said in my sweetest voice, 'Where are you?'

Holy crap! I find Cedric…the Rottweiler …very protectively guarding the biggest bone I have ever seen.

At this point I was concerned not only for my safety, but also that I'm looking at the remnants of the previous Good Samaritan sent in to get him. The little biscuit I had quivering in my hand would be no consolation should I somehow manage to get the bone away. The look on *'little'* Cedric's face also told me that he had good dental hygiene as he bared his teeth in a display of sheer aggression telling me to back off. I have to admit at this point I think I may have peed slightly as I made a hasty retreat, backside first.

'Did you find him dear? Is he okay?' What I wanted to say was, *'Little Cedric? What the hell do you mean little? He has muscles that Arnold Schwarzenegger can only dream of! How in God's name do you expect me to pull out a ten ton Rottweiler chewing some poor sod's femur?'*

But what I actually said was,

'Oh, he's fine. He's just having a little chew on a bone he's found. I don't think I can get it off him, but I'm sure he'll come out as soon as he's finished it.'

I thought about asking if he lived at the local old people's home and whether they had checked all the residents, but I thought this may be a bit much for the poor old boy. I made a hasty retreat from the field with muddy knees, scratched arms and slightly damp knickers. So much for helping out.

Anyway, back to my story. On deciding to move out, the first trauma I had was to find somewhere to rent that allowed dogs. Bloody hell, I went to visit some dumps; to say that they were shitholes would be like saying that Beirut needs a bit of building work. One particularly noteworthy place was described in the advert as a 'small self-contained fully furnished flat close to the shops and local amenities'. So I turned up there, friend in tow, hoping that this was just what I was looking for. The pictures looked great, the price was right and it was located not too far from work. All good. How wrong could I have been?

First of all, actually finding it was a challenge. Anybody who knows me will tell you that I don't have the best sense of direction, this will become apparent as I recount more tales. However, on this occasion I was armed with directions, a map and my trusty navigator friend Laura, but still we must have scoured the area for 20 minutes looking for it. When we did eventually stumble upon it, no wonder we'd struggled. The 'small flat' was actually a prefab type building sat in somebody's overgrown back yard with the only access through a narrow ginnel.

At this point I knew the place wasn't for me but as I'd arranged to meet somebody there it seemed rude not to turn up and, to be quite honest, curiosity to see what the inside was like got the better of me. If I was being nice I could say that the inside was dated, but if I was being honest the inside could have been used for a remake of *Steptoe and Son*. Having got past the 'water feature' in the yard…the rusting hosepipe reel …we entered the prefab.

Now, bearing in mind I'd seen photos of this

place, it was not unreasonable to have some expectations. If you ever want photos taking I can recommend the photographer. I'm sure he could make you look a million dollars even if you had no make-up on, hair like a bird's nest and a spot the size of a boiled egg on your face.

Although it was indeed fully furnished, I don't think co-ordination was a word they understood unless you thought orange, cerise pink and maroon are a match made in heaven. The sofa was something out of a 1960s farmhouse being a rustic maroon and gold colour with tassels around the cushions, whilst the table had been bought from Ikea for a children's playroom. Hmm… obviously a reject from a now grown up child.

An attempt had been made to modernise the kitchen, although the fridge-freezer, now located in the lounge, was again on the dated side, you could almost say retro if you were being generous and overlooked the dents in the sides. I won't go into the details of the bedroom but all I will say is the stains on the mattress were questionable to say the least. I've seen enough episodes of *CSI* to know that they weren't tea or coffee.

The person showing us around was the owner's father, a pleasant enough bloke if you ignored the tattoos across the knuckles that said 'love' and 'hat'. Yes, he did have a finger missing. Either that or he was a milliner.

Having been taken on the tour we made our escape saying that we would let them know. I took the coward's way out later by sending them a text saying that unfortunately it was not what I was looking for, but failed to add 'unless I'm looking for a musty smelling dump decorated by a colour-blind misfit'.

I did eventually find a very nice little one-bedroom house on the outskirts of Knutsford that had been newly decorated and was perfect for me and Ferdinand to start our new life.

2

Bin Here Long?

The house I'd rented was a small, one up one down, which may seem a bit odd. The only way I can describe it to you is that you take two normal semis and halve them widthways to make four adjoining houses. Strange I know; this meant I had three neighbours. My new home was lovely and cosy, being just the right size for me and Ferdinand, but my only complaint would be that the walls were way too thin.

When I first moved into my tissue paper house, there was a nice young couple who lived behind me, a bloke at the side of me and a young girl diagonal to me. So, as the walls had been made from papier-mache and sticky-back plastic, you could hear quite a bit of what went on. Before I even got to meet the fellow next door I had the pleasure of being able to listen to him snoring every night. Some nights it sounded like a drunken *Peppa Pig* was being molested by *Suzi Sheep* equipped with a pneumatic drill. Even worse than the snoring though was the flatulence. My God, could that bloke fart! I had considered popping a load of Wind-eze through his door with a note attached saying, 'For Christ sake, eat me!'

When I did eventually come face to face with the one-man wind section from number 19 though, I'm not sure what he thought of this new neighbour.

Let me set the scene for you: I'd been living in my new home for a few weeks when, after a thorough vacuuming to get rid of the copious amount of hair, both dog and blonde, the hoover needed emptying. I'm not sure who sheds more but at this rate, I'd be able to make a decent wig for Donald Trump. I'd only recently bought the hoover, which was one of the bag-less varieties that you just empty out. As I tipped all the dust and hair out into my wheelie bin, the hoover sort of… fell apart, and the contents, along with the filter, plummeted into the recently emptied bin. Needless to say, it plunged right to the bottom. Shit!

Now being an intelligent individual I thought, *'I know I'll stand on the doorstep and this will give me better reach to get to the bottom of the bin'*. Hmmm… What it actually gave me was more leverage to propel myself IN, and slightly less gracefully than Tom Daley off a three-meter spring board too. I ended up head first in the upright bin with my doggy slippers waggling out of the top for all to see, while I mumbled expletives from the bottom of the bin. As I couldn't push myself out, I rocked the bin to try and get it to tip over. You can now imagine the scene, doggy slippers and a rocking bin; it looked like some perverse children's puppet show.

I eventually managed to rock my way over only to emerge to face my new neighbour who was clearly concerned but highly amused. I'm sure he had never seen anything quite like the crimson faced dusty blonde before him holding a hoover filter. Yep, first impressions are definitely better when you don't look like something dug up from *Raiders of the Lost Ark* in doggy slippers.

Emptying the hoover wasn't the only simple task that caused me to question my ability to function on my own. Take buying an ironing board, or fitting a smoke alarm for instance. Simple chores, am I right? Yes, that's exactly what I thought, but when you've also turned into somebody with the brain of a dazed camel, it's not as straightforward as you would think.

When I moved into the house I realised that I didn't have either of these crucial pieces of kit. Let's look at the simplest of these two tasks first shall we? Buying an ironing board. A definite plus of being on my own was that I now had merely a molehill of ironing to do in comparison with the pile the height of Kilimanjaro I previously had, but nevertheless I still needed something to iron on.

Have you ever bought an ironing board in a supermarket? No? Well don't. They don't fit in the trolley properly and you can guarantee you get the one with a dodgy wheel. You then have the task of negotiating your way around the aisles with the board sticking out of the top as you try desperately to avoid the displays. Or NOT in my case. Just as I turned the unwieldy contraption I clipped the 'On Offer' display. A minor clip…. nothing broken. Just a few hundred bottles of Flash and Vanish scattered on the floor causing blockages and trolleys to back up in neighbouring aisles. No big deal eh? On the plus side, at least the assistant didn't have to go and get anything to clean the floor with.

Then, let's consider the fitting of a smoke alarm. Although it's important that every house should be equipped with one, I have to confess that the reason it became apparent that this was an essential addition to the fixtures and fittings, was that I successfully managed to incinerate a couple of dinners that could have resulted in a trip to the pharmacy at best, or A&E at worst.

The worst of my cremated creations was some garlic bread, simple enough to cook even if you have the culinary skills of a two-year-old surely? I've cooked three course meals, Christmas dinners and the odd barbecue or two, so garlic bread would be a cinch, right? I put the electric oven on and popped the bread in, I even remembered to set the timer as instructed.

Safe in the knowledge that I would be alerted once it looked as mouth-watering as the packet depicted, I nipped upstairs to do some ironing on my newly acquired board. This was proving quite a challenge as it had clearly been designed by a Mensa candidate, with the awkward contraption at the back rivalling the Rubik's cube in complexity. This meant that by the time I'd fiddled away with the release mechanism, like a teenage boy fumbling to unfasten his first bra strap, the timer was ready for going off. The moment I heard the repetitive beeping, I threw down the board in defeat and returned downstairs. Unfortunately, as I entered the lounge I was met with smoke billowing...yes billowing, from under the kitchen door!

Flaming hell! I felt like I was in an episode of *London's Burning* as I dashed into the kitchen, choked my way through the doorway and flung the oven door open to be confronted with the blackest piece of garlic bread I had ever seen. Bugger! My tea now resembled a piece of charcoal so black you would be scraping bits out your teeth for weeks. You'd give the lead singer of The Pogues a run for his money in the Dental Disasters Top Twenty. It was so bad I even took a picture of it for posterity. It was a bit like playing *Ask the Family* getting people to identify what it was. I later realised my little faux pas had been that instead of putting the oven on, what I had actually done was put the grill on which meant the butter on the garlic bread had quickly burnt to generate enough smoke to rival Deirdre Barlow's living room.

So, after that, a hasty trip to B&Q was required to buy a smoke alarm. Now as I'm no expert in DIY, I decided that the best thing to do was to stick it up rather than attempt to screw it into the ceiling. I'm not talking a Pritt Stick here, no I mean the hard-core stuff designed to stick a small, unruly child to the wall. Not that I've ever tested this. Mind you, I can't deny I've been tempted a few times with other people's offspring, especially when they run around pubs while their parents get increasingly rat-arsed whilst telling the little buggers to, 'Piss off and play and stop fucking bothering me'. Anyway, having purchased the smoke alarm and industrial strength tape, I returned home to stick the smoke alarm to the ceiling. PERFECT. Well it was until 3 o'clock in the morning when it came crashing down, smashed on the floor and set Ferdinand off into a frantic barking spree. I can't imagine this went down well with the new neighbours as the sound reverberated through their walls.

You will be pleased to know I did buy another one, and this time managed to screw it into the ceiling with no mishaps. Wahoo …DIY Goddess.

Still, the racket created by Ferdinand in his attempt to wake the sleeping neighbourhood and alert them to the broken alarm, was not quite as bad as the disturbances the woman over the road, whom I have aptly named Sweary Mary, had to put up with on a regular basis. The fella next door to her would frequently bring back ladies of the night or 'fucking prostitutes' as she so eloquently put it.

When I first moved in, she strode across to kindly introduce herself and immediately launched into a tirade of,

'The walls are fucking thin in these houses, aren't they? I had to tell the bloke that used to live next to me to stop fucking shagging so much because I can hear every wheeze and fucking grunt!'

Erm Okaaayyy. Nice to meet you too! There is not a lot you can say to that other than, 'Oh really'.

'Yeah,' she went on, 'I said if he didn't fucking keep the noise down when he's getting his end away I would record it and play it to everybody.' I'm not sure who everybody was, but I doubted they'd be adding it to their playlist...unless of course you like to listen to Puff Daddy followed by Puffed Out.

Being as I am, the sort of overly polite person who attracts the mentally unstable, Sweary Mary then made it her mission to take me on a tour of the local area. We were also accompanied by her pug-nosed hairy shiatsu. Great. I now had to go on a walk with a verbally abusive woman and her gender confused mop of a dog called Trixie... It's a boy!

When I first saw her, I thought she had a bit of a limp, as she always seemed to have a stick with her. But no. As I found out on our stroll, whenever any large dog came within butt sniffing distance of her little Trixie, she shook the stick and told the owner to, 'Get your fucking dog under control'.

Oh-Oh. Nutter alert! No wonder people gave her a wider berth than a leper giving out condoms. Unluckily, she had taken a definite shine to me as, despite making excuses to avoid being associated with this obviously insane woman, she then offered to take me tap dancing. Oh joy. She now considered herself my best mate. Apparently, she tripped the light fantastic each week with a local dance troop, putting dents in the parquet flooring at the church hall. I had visions of her using steel toe-capped boots instead of tap shoes with the sole purpose of being able to kick the living daylights out of somebody in the pretence she was performing a heel-toe shuffle. Obviously, I declined this kind offer making some feeble excuse about having two left feet and a rare condition where I couldn't listen to repetitive tapping without breaking into a sweat. I even told her that I once had a panic attack watching *42nd Street* and had to be carried out of the theatre having fainted in my popcorn bucket.

Undeterred to make me her new best friend, she then offered to come away with me; well when I say offered, to my ears it sounded more like a threat. I was loading the car one day, ready to set off for a couple of days of peace and quiet away from the hullabaloo of my hectic life, when over she stomps, mop in tow.

'I'll come with you one time.' she said, 'We'll have a fucking great time.' Eeek. There was none of this, 'Could I come with you?' which normal sane but still pushy people would have said. Oh no; she was *telling* me she was coming with me. Shit! How do I get out of this now? That's it, I thought, I am now going to have to load the car surreptitiously in the middle of the night to avoid spending an entire weekend being cooped up with this verbally aggressive crazy person.

So, there you have it. That was my new start. My nights were filled with echoes of trumping and snoring, my cooking came with a health warning and trips away now took on a challenge worthy of the *Great Escape*.

3

Cross County and Cross Trainers

To be a truly independent woman it helps to have a good sense of direction. Unfortunately, this particular inherent characteristic was left in the gene pool swimming away happily with my common sense. I can't say that this tendency to get lost is a recent development though. For me, a total lack of a directional awareness is. I couldn't find my way out of a one-way street with a map, compass and breadcrumbs to follow. If I were Gretel, I would still be in the woods chomping my way through the gingerbread house.

I've lost count of the number of times I've been late for work meetings. This is never down to not giving myself enough time, well, I suppose technically it is but, if I were to take into account getting lost every time, I would need to set off a day earlier packing an emergency bivvy bag to sleep in, and a flask…just in case. If I had written *Around the World in 80 Days* it would have been entitled *Around and Around the World in 160 Days via the Bit Nobody Ever Visits Unless Lost*. Snappy title eh?

There was one occasion where I arrived in Glasgow for a meeting with a customer a whole hour and a half early; all I had to do was find the building. I drove round the sights of Glasgow, and then drove round the sights of Glasgow again.

Glasgow is a very lovely architectural city with lots of stunning buildings but on the third time of passing the same street and the same drunk on the corner, I decided enough was enough and I stopped to ask where I was. I am a woman after all so I do ask for directions… eventually.

I spotted a friendly looking postman. Nobody better I thought. He'll know where the building is. Having pulled over to the side of the busy road to the sound of beeps and some garbled swear words, I politely asked where I could find the address in question.

'Och yurrr bluedy malls awey lass. Yar ned ti gow back dune this rod and tak a leeft at the lats. Drav fur aboot a mall and yall see a boos depo. Its jus past thear on the rat.'

Hmmm…Okay! I said thanks and then tried to decipher and remember what he'd said. It's never easy driving in a major city but when you've been given directions in what seems like a foreign language it's even harder. Can you imagine the carnage if Scotland drove on the opposite side of the road? I did eventually end up at the 'boos depo', or should I say IN it. However, as I was not driving a double-decker bus (Thank God, I hear you mumble), I was getting many an odd look not to mention a few beeps as I pulled in behind the X25 ready to depart for Cumbernauld. Not wanting the awaiting passengers with their bags of shopping piling into my Vauxhall Corsa, I made a quick exit, but after another 30 minutes and yet another tour of Glasgow along the same streets, I decided I would have to give in. The drunk, meanwhile, had been admitted to rehab thinking he was experiencing *Groundhog Day* for the fourth time.

On passing the nearest car park, I parked up and decided I would have to get a taxi to the building. Finding a taxi was a cinch, he did however give me a strange look when I told him the address. He drove around the corner and then after a few yards down the road, he stopped. He had a little chuckle as he saw the look on my face, he didn't charge me saying,

'Och yur feen lass, it's on the hewse'. It was a shame the car park didn't have the same policy; it cost me a bloody fortune to park for the day not to mention the tank of fuel driving around.

Getting lost isn't restricted to journeys further afield; I even managed to get lost on my way home from work once. I'd decided to go a different way as I needed to pick up some new walking trousers; it wasn't exactly *en route* but only required a small deviation to get there. Having missed the initial turning, I took the next road thinking it ran parallel. It didn't. I ended up in a housing estate and then a business park. I swear there were skeletons of other lost souls who had wandered or driven in by mistake never to be seen again.

They're like mazes those new estates. If they all put hedges in their front gardens they could charge you an entrance fee and only provide you with a map and a bottle of water if you paid an exorbitant fee to the unscrupulous entrepreneur in the middle advertising *Escape Routes*.

Driving is not the only time I find myself saying, 'Where the hell am I?' I like to keep fit by walking Ferdinand, but as I have the sense of direction of a blind hamster, I decided it would be wiser to join a gym instead. Even I can't get lost on a cross trainer, or cross dresser as my Mum calls it. This always conjures up an image of some big hairy bloke in a cerise pink spandex leotard sweating away to "I am what I am" while chatting about how you can't get Jimmy Choo's in size 11s for love nor money.

I've never really been one for going to the gym but, as I work in an office and I'm sat on my backside all day, I was beginning to feel that my posterior was starting to resemble a couple of large suet puddings after ten hours on the boil. It also seemed like a good way to meet new people as well as get fit.

Before going to the session though I first had to purchase a new pair of trainers; the only pair I owned had been used for dog walking and were fashionable when you used to wear leg warmers with them. Okay I'm exaggerating slightly but they were old and tatty so were completely unsuitable for using in a gym. I could just imagine turning up in my mud-stained footwear, only to receive snooty looks from the gleaming trainer brigade.

My God, there are so many trainers to choose from. Some are so expensive you'd need to get a mortgage or sell a kidney. I obviously didn't go for the top of the range, well I couldn't get a mortgage and I needed all my organs, so I just went for the special offer glowing white ones. They would do, after all it was only the gym, it's not like I was planning to take on Paula Radcliffe just yet. I don't think I could beat her in the *Take a Dump in the Most Public Place* competition either unless I decided to unload myself in front of a traffic cam on the M25 in rush hour.

As with any new gym membership though, before being let loose on any equipment, you first have to go through the obligatory medical session where you subject yourself to more questions than when you get admitted to hospital. I was waiting to be given a bottle to provide a sample in and asked how many sexual partners I'd had, it was that intense. No wonder my blood pressure was a bit high, I felt like I was an overweight unhealthy alcoholic by the time I came out. At least with my new footwear though I felt the part, well until you looked at the scruffy shorts and t-shirt that I'd grabbed at the last minute. I thought it was a plain white one but unfortunately, I'd picked up an old *Children in Need* one I wear for doing the cleaning in.

Following the full health check-up, you are then given an introductory session by one of the fitness instructors. I bet you're thinking that I wanted some gorgeous young hunk to take me through my paces for my induction, bearing in mind the initial comment about hornyness aren't you? But on this occasion, I was hoping for some nice girl that I wouldn't feel like a total buffoon next to as I got a sweat on just getting on and off the treadmill. But do you ever get what you want in this life? Nope. I ended up with the fit young hunk. Typical. Where's a fat sweaty bloke when you need him?

So here I was looking like some charity sports runner reject while 'Tony' on the other hand looked like a Greek god: a six pack you wouldn't get from Bargain Booze, biceps that were so toned you could bounce a boiled egg off them, a tight bum that looked like a couple of bowling balls in his shorts and thighs that made you sweat just thinking about being between them.

For a woman in her forties, I don't have the worst body in the world, apart from the wobbly pudding bum, but obviously there are lots of things I'd change. Well who wouldn't? I've always wanted bigger boobs and longer legs but, unfortunately even if I went to the gym 24/7 and ate nothing but celery while I rowed my way to Canada and back, it wouldn't make any difference to these two things. So, when Tony asked me,

'What do you want to get out of your sessions?' all I could come up with was,

'Oh, I dunno, maybe a bit of toning and build my STANIMA'. I could see a little smirk on his face as he said,

'Erm right. Just general fitness then?'

Determined that he wouldn't think I was a complete moron of the highest order I repeated,

'Yep especially my STANIMA'. What was wrong with me for God's sake? Why did I not just shut up! Great. He now thinks I'm some scruffy unfit woman with the fashion sense of a vagrant and a speech impediment.

He began to take me round all the different pieces of equipment, explaining what each one was for, some I have to say wouldn't look out of place in scenes from the Spanish Inquisition.

I bet if aliens came down to earth and landed in Fitness First they'd think we were a very strange species indeed, all running away like little gerbils on treadmills not going anywhere or grunting like constipated yaks as we lifted weights. God forbid they went to a zumba class. Have you ever been to one? It's like a Friday night out with a load of women jiggling about in supportive bras with the odd bit of wind escaping as the jumping gets into full swing. I reckon they would take one look and soon come to the conclusion that the air on this planet so addles your brain they would be out of there quicker than we could say *ET Go Home*.

As I made my way around the equipment with toned Tony, all was going well. No more verbal dyslexia and I even managed to take in the instructions whilst being distracted by his flexing biceps.

We then came to a contraption that is for toning your tummy; just what I needed. Now how to describe this to you so you get the picture? Hmmm. Think a sort of pulley system for the Pope. I'll explain: you're on your knees holding onto two handles at shoulder height that are attached to ropes with weights at the end. As you lean forward, the weights support you as you go into prayer mode. You then use your stomach muscles to pull yourself upright, once again supported by the ropes and weights. You are not, however, meant to put your whole body weight into it but use muscles to support yourself.

As I knelt down and leant forward the weights that were on the end were obviously not enough to support me; I fell face first in to the floor as if I had drunk all the communal wine. Fuck! I lay there for a moment in stunned silence while I stared at the carpet. Fortunately, the angle I landed at meant that I hit my forehead first and not my nose.

'Oh my God, are you alright?' said Tony. *No, I'm bloody not alright. I've just done a head dive into the floor in front of a sex god of a gym instructor. He now not only thinks I'm a stupid woman who can't say stamina and is a member of the Pudsey Fan Club, but is also some weird prayer nut that head-butts the floor.*

'Erm. Yes. I think so, thanks'.

I stood up trying to get back a modicum of dignity, but this was not helped by Tony holding my arms like he was escorting his granny around the supermarket. As I passed a mirror in a slightly dazed state, I could see a big red bump had developed on my forehead.

Marvellous! How attractive! With the pale face, the sweat plastered hair and slightly run mascara. Alice Cooper eat your heart out.

The rest of the demonstration was now put on hold for fear of concussion, although I think Tony was more worried I was going to sue the gym for disfigurement.

I've only been back to the gym a few times since, always avoiding the prayer contraption. I have to confess that I do find them really dull and, despite trying to tell myself it will do me good, I just can't muster up the enthusiasm to go.

The classes are a bit better, the belly dancing class was my particular favourite; yes *belly* not ballet. I can't imagine a bunch of slightly flabby women predominantly in their 40s doing pirouettes and pliés in pink tutus to *Swan Lake*, can you? It would look more like emus on *Golden Pond*.

Belly dancing however, is enormous fun as long as you don't take it too seriously and as a bonus it's a great way to get fit. All that Far Eastern jiggling about and hip movement may make you look like you've just been electrocuted with a cattle prod, but it's fantastic exercise.

Despite my best efforts to not look like a swaying *Teletubby*, I was always getting shouted at as apparently it helps to have feet flatter than a steam-rollered pancake. Every time I lifted a heel one fraction of a millimetre off the floor, the belly-dancing commandant, who was masquerading as the instructor, would yell, 'Get those feet flat' in a way that made me think I'd joined the armed forces rather than an exercise class. She was a bit excessive, and way too serious, with an attitude and face that would intimidate Vinny Jones and my God, she had the hairiest legs I'd ever seen outside of the gorilla enclosure at Whipsnade.

It wasn't like we were thinking of taking it up professionally to give a belly wobbling performance at the local Turkish while people ate their falafel on a Friday night. The problem was that the more she barked her instructions revealing her annoyance at my lack of commitment, the more it made me laugh. And I wasn't the only one. Instead of inspiring the next bunch of Shakiras to shake their hips like they don't lie, what she actually got was a bunch of giggly sweaty women wobbling their way flat-footed round the dance studio looking more like a drunken physiotherapy class…. post hip replacement.

4

Good Vibrations

I've mentioned that my thinking capabilities diminished to the equivalent of a sleep deprived sloth, but the opposite happened to my sex drive: my libido hit an all-time high. I actually thought at one point I was turning into a man with every other thought being about sex. I didn't have the equivalent desire to scratch my crotch and fart after every meal, but this new obsession with sex definitely seemed like male thinking.

Other than some much needed DIY and no, I am not talking a quick trip to B&Q to get some drill bits and a compression valve, I was getting no release from this pent up hornyness. So, after much deliberation I decided the time had come to invest in something that would help. As George Clooney was not available my thoughts turned to purchasing a vibrator.

Don't get me wrong I didn't suddenly wake up one day, sit on the washer and look at a cucumber in the fridge and think, *I know what I need*. No; the realisation that vibrators were no longer something to hide in the wardrobe with the Shakin' Stevens records and the collection of ornamental poodles your grandmother passed down to you, came after a drunken weekend with a friend. I hadn't realised that so many women had them; no wonder Duracell kept in business! It's not like I had led a sheltered life but you just didn't talk about these things. I've never been one to watch *Loose Women* either… Well I work for one thing and this programme, along with *The Jeremy Kyle Show*, have always seemed like viewing for the redundant, the bored, or the benefit brigade.

Once I'd decided a vibrator was what I needed, a shopping trip to Anne Summers was arranged with my friend Claire. I'd never been in this shop before; just looking in the window had made me go as red as some of the knickers on display, so before the trip to purchase said item, a quick wine or two was required at the nearby bar in the Trafford Centre for a bit of Dutch courage. It's amazing the difference a glass of vino can make to a girl's confidence as I entered the shop head held high and not a red cheek in sight.

When I got in there I found it was just like walking into any nice underwear shop. Blimey, they had some really nice items and not a bit kinky; this however lulled me into a false sense of security. Once safely past the undergarments we wandered around nonchalantly pretending we knew what we were looking for, and found ourselves in the uniform and costume section. Hmmm. That was an eye opener. I'm sure that if our brave and dedicated police officers wore such revealing rubber uniforms a few more criminals would be taken off the streets just for the pleasure of being arrested. A new policy for you there Mr Chief Constable.

We eventually got to the sex toys section, where there was such an array of objects on display, some of which would make your eyes water and others, well I'll be honest, I hadn't a clue what they were. Now you have to remember we are two mature, supposedly sensible women, not a couple of silly teenagers, so the idea was to just find what I wanted and get out of there. But the evils of wine combined with an element of nervousness had taken effect and we started to giggle like a couple of virgins leafing through the male underwear section of a catalogue. Go on, admit it. You know that's what you did as a teenager when the Littlewoods catalogue dropped through the door.

As wine bravery took over we quickly made a beeline for the display table where there were a large number of vibrators… I was going to say available to test, but I think *that* idea is just wrong. I went to pick up an item that I thought was meant to resemble a finger, although if anybody had fingers like that they would seriously struggle getting gloves to fit and they'd certainly struggle texting, it was HUGE.

Claire selected a neat little vibrator, opting for the more discrete version. However, as she switched it on it started to vibrate, not surprisingly, and made quite a loud buzzing noise for such a small thing. This caught the attention of a passing couple nervously browsing the shelves. They were quite a bit older and clearly just as inexperienced and uncomfortable in this shop as we were. The woman was wearing a pleated skirt that rested just under her boobs, which were trying to escape from under a lovely nylon green cardigan, and the man was in an anorak and hush puppies. Think Mrs Merton and Roy Cropper. They would've looked more at home in the library than a sex shop. She had clearly read *Fifty Shades of Grey* and decided they needed to spice things up a bit. By the look on the bloke's face I had a feeling that he would have preferred to have been shopping in Tesco followed by *Match of the Day* and a cup of cocoa.

As the noise reverberated around the immediate area like a bee caught in a glass, the woman had the look of a startled rabbit in headlights and quickly moved away while the bloke tried to hide, appropriately behind a display of gimp masks.

When I get nervous I start to laugh. I can't help it, so as Claire tried desperately to switch it off, all I could do was giggle. However, instead of stopping the thing she managed to make it go faster and faster and with this the buzzing got louder and louder.... It now sounded like a very irate bee in a glass. At this point Claire was redder than a baboon's bum and all I could do was laugh hysterically.

'Oh God! Just put it on the table and walk away!' I said. This was not the wisest bit of advice I could've given. Anybody with an ounce of common sense would know that as soon as she placed the violently vibrating little bugger down it immediately started to quickly move across the table making its escape quicker than Lance Armstrong at the drug test centre. And Oh. My. God. The noise. It had turned into a swarm of pissed off bees. I quickly grabbed the little devil before it plunged off the end of the table like a torpedo in a nose dive, but in my haste to stop the noise I somehow managed to pull the bottom off. Ahhhhhh… Silence.

The only problem was that by now all the people in the shop were looking at us as I stood there with a bright pink vibrator in two pieces in my hand. Claire left the scene sharpish but I could still hear her behind the gimp display giggling like a five-year-old. There is nothing quite like the support of a friend in an embarrassing situation, and this was nothing like support.

At this point the assistant had seen enough and took pity on me coming over to help. The smirk on her face told me that watching people embarrass themselves as they played with the toys was how she made the day go quicker. I'm still convinced it was rigged to not switch off.

Having removed the two-piece vibrator from my sweaty hands she asked if she could help in any way? 'Yes please.' I squeaked in a strangled high-pitched voice. So, without further ado she started to talk me through some of the toys available. Claire, had actually managed to control her laughter at this point and slunk back to listen with interest as the assistant explained the items. Claire was particularly taken with a Cock and

Bollocks vibrator that you stuck in the shower. It looked a bit like a large towel hook and the thoughts of her mother-in-law's face next time she visited and took her towel off proved a bit too much to take so we both started to giggle again.

The assistant tutted like we were a couple of irritating kids but carried on taking us through the vibrators available. They had large and small, thick or thin, ones that rotated and ones that pulsated, some that were long and some that were short. They had different speeds and different motions, there were bumps and ball- bearings or just plain huge, but above all they all guaranteed one thing…satisfaction.

After much deliberation, I opted to go for the slim but perfectly formed bunny, I didn't feel the need to go for the eye watering colossal one. After all size isn't important, right?

Once I'd made the purchase, I double-wrapped the Anne Summers bag in a more acceptable M&S carrier. Well you never know who you might meet. God forbid I would see somebody from work; the news would be round the office quicker than the leaving collection for the miserable bastard who never speaks to anybody, picks his nose at the desk and smells of fag ends.

Now I'm not going to go into details of when I used my vibrator Vernon as I like to call him, but I will say one thing: for any ladies out there wondering if it was worth it? I can honestly say that it was the best £38 I ever spent.

5

Next Stop the Olympics!

I've always been relatively fit, mainly due to the numerous weekends spent walking in the Lake District during my married life. If you've never been you should give it a go as it's one of the most beautiful places in the world; especially if you think a cagoule is the height of fashion.

We were fortunate enough to be able to afford a caravan up there so, for 14 wonderful years, we spent many weekends as a family either walking, water-skiing or just spending evenings with friends we made. This usually involved a few drinks sitting out under a patio heater or brolly. It is the Lake District after all.

My son, Adam, had a great childhood with the freedom to go off with friends on his bike and make dens in the woods. I don't think that they'd have passed any housing standards but they did just fine for a group of young boys looking for somewhere to eat chocolate, get giddy on Lucozade and talk *Top Gear*. As he got older the prospect of being dragged up a hill became about as appealing as attending a double history lesson with Mr Knowles who was renowned for having the personality of a dead cat, a Brummie accent that could send you to sleep quicker than a dose of Night Nurse, and an unhealthy obsession of talking about the battle re-enactments that he regularly attended. He actually got the sack in the end as a number of parents complained when he brought in his musket and scared the kids shitless by pretending to load and fire it. Obviously all the sniffing gunpowder and wearing hessian pants had taken its toll.

Anyway, whenever we did manage to drag Adam on a ramble, he was always 'soooooo tired' while we were out, but then as soon as we got back he was off with the renewed energy of a wind turbine in a high wind. We wouldn't see him for hours until hunger took over and he would be back complaining he was 'staaaarving'. This was a fabulous time in my life and one I would never change.

For a while after we separated we kept the place in the Lakes and I still loved to go on my own with Ferdinand although, without my trusty Sherpa of a husband, I limited walks to the ones I was familiar with. I didn't want to risk being one of those people on the programme *Mountain Rescue* where they end up lost up a hill in the dead of night with nothing but an empty water bottle and a six-month-old cereal bar that was hidden at the bottom of the rucksack. I used to think what would happen if Ferdinand injured himself, could I call mountain rescue out? I had this image of having to carry him in my rucksack, ears flapping behind like an ugly big-nosed child in a papoose.

Although Ferdinand usually accompanied me on my trips, there were a few times when I went with friends; these weekends usually involved more time in the pubs than on the hills. We'd always walk to the pub to make us feel better about sitting there all afternoon getting slowly inebriated. Funny though, we never really felt the urge to walk back. It was probably for the best though, as it would take twice as long and then there was the awful prospect of wanting to pee halfway back to consider.

Yep, that's another thing that goes when you reach a certain age…bladder control. I used to have the bladder capacity of a donkey, but now I can't pass a toilet without having to nip in to check out the facilities. I don't always need to go but you just never know when you'll next pass one do you? When I go on long hikes I drink next to nothing just in case. Knowing my luck, I'll be squatting, knickers and walking trousers around my ankles, only partially hidden by a prickly gorse bush, trying to concentrate on not peeing on my boots, when a large school party will traipse past. I don't think a wobbly white backside will be on their list of *Things in the Countryside to Look out For*.

On a lovely sunny day though, there's nothing better than sitting by the lake with a bottle of wine, or jug of Pimms, watching the boats go by. Some of them are so big and expensive, they would look much better anchored in crystal-clear sea off some gorgeous Greek island complete with a bikini-clad babe sunbathing on the front whilst sipping a glass of chilled champagne. Here in the Lakes, they are moored on a bird shit covered buoy in the freezing rain with an anorak clad figure supping from a flask. These people obviously have the money for the boat but are about as confident at navigating the high seas as Captain Pugwash and his merry band of reprobates. It seems much safer to tootle round a lake where the worst thing that can happen is that after a few beers you swear that you saw Windermere's equivalent to the Loch Ness monster, Bownessy, but then actually turns out to be nothing more than a large branch off a tree.

Over the years many a bottle of wine has been consumed on a lovely evening down at the jetties on the caravan site watching the sunset. The only problem was the bloody midges. You'd be sat there quietly enjoying the view and a glass of vino, when all of a sudden they'd appear out of nowhere in their thousands, swarming round you like a cloud of tiny blood-sucking ninjas. I swear they see me as some sort of all-you-can-eat buffet. Some nights following a lakeside session my face would look like a dot-to-dot. I once joined them all up with an eye pencil and it looked remarkably like a small elephant ..after a few wines obviously!

One sunny weekend when I was there with three friends, we were feeling particularly inspired by the rare hot weather and the beautiful lake, as well as a few glasses of wine, so decided to try our hand at cruising the waters. Well, when I say 'cruising' this probably conjures up an image of a boat of some sort. What we actually decided to do was take out a dinghy we had stored under the caravan. We didn't have visions of giving Sir Steve Redgrave a run for his money, but thought it would be good fun to just row around the jetties.

Although fairly sturdy by dinghy standards, it could really only hold two adults. As we couldn't all pile in, Claire and I, being the smallest and stupidest of the group, decided to test the waters so to speak. Not wanting to go too far we decided to just row out to a tired-looking boat covered in seagull poo that was moored just off the jetties and then come back. A nice short trip and we had life jackets. What could go wrong?

You're probably thinking that we fell getting in the boat or it tipped up, aren't you? But no, we eased ourselves into the dinghy like a couple of boating pros. Once successfully settled in the dinghy we set off rowing to our target destination. I don't think Sir Steve would have been impressed with my rowing skills that's for sure, as we went around in more circles than a dog with distemper and then took a meandering course that made the Monaco Grand Prix course look like Route 66 in comparison. As you can imagine, having the paddling abilities of a one-armed pirate was causing much hilarity for the girls on shore, I don't know what ached more, my arms from rowing or my stomach from laughing.

I rowed for what felt like five miles, Sir Steve

would have been at the other end of the lake by now having a rub down and reading *Regatta Weekly* in the time it took us to reach the crap-covered boat. As I had been doing all the hard work while Claire, the lazy bugger, sat back and enjoyed the sunshine, I decided it was now time to change over to give my tired little arms a much needed break; if I carried on I was in danger of not being able to lift my glass of wine later! Unfortunately, as we swapped over the oars, in what should have been an easy manoeuvre, Claire (I'm going to blame her here as it is me that is writing this so I have author's privilege) didn't grab hold of one of the oars properly so it gently slid through the loop and into the lake quicker than a ferret down a rabbit hole. 'Oh shit' we said simultaneously as we watched it float away out of reach.

Claire immediately went into panic mode, 'Oh My God! What are we going to do?' she said as she flapped her arms like that was going to miraculously bring the oar back. 'Bloody sit still for a start you daft cow or you'll tip us over.' I said for fear that her impression of a demented ostrich trying to get airborne was going to plummet us both into the lake. 'We can reach it with the other one…we just need to try and move a bit nearer.'

So, whilst doing a very bad impression of Hiawatha, I began to attempt to paddle us towards the drifting oar as Claire tentatively tried to reach over the side to grab it. Unfortunately, as we made slow headway, the elusive oar, propelled by the gods of *'Bugger you'*, was much quicker at making its escape.

'It's no good. I can't get to it.' Claire whinged stating the bloody obvious.

'Oh bugger it, I'll just have to go in and get it,' I said, after all I did my bronze swimming medal at school where you had to swim a length and tread water in your pyjamas, so swimming in the lake in shorts and t-shirt should be a cinch, I wouldn't even have to dive for a rubber brick in the process.

I gently eased myself over the side trying not to tip the whole dinghy over and gracefully immersed myself in the water with the skill of a pearl diver. Oh okay, I plopped over the side,

'Holy crap! It's bloody freezing!' I howled as I flailed about like a catch of the day.

Even on the hottest day of the year Lake Windermere still manages to maintain its sub-zero status, but once I became accustomed to the arctic-like temperatures that would not only freeze the balls on a brass monkey but also turn the rest of him into an ice cube, I grabbed onto the ropes around the dinghy and pulled us toward the now distant oar.

I'm quite a strong swimmer, having gone to a swimming club for many years as a child. Every Wednesday night and Sunday morning I went with my sister, Katy, Mum and Dad to a pool that was part of the university campus near where we lived. It was quite a nice pool, although a bit on the cold side. I think they kept the temperature low so you couldn't linger in there too long without ending up looking like a chattering Smurf in a bathing suit.

They had the usual poolside sign warnings: 'No petting, diving or jumping allowed'. Who on earth thought of putting petting in the list of Don'ts? Surely there are worse things you could do in a pool? Peeing for one thing. They also had the obligatory oddball characters in the swimming club which was open to anybody who was willing to pay the nominal weekly subscription. I think this went to maintaining the student bar rather than the pool. It certainly wasn't used to heat the bloody thing.

I remember one particularly bizarre, but lovely lady, called Maureen who used to smother her face with Nivea and put talcum powder under her extremely hairy armpits *before* she went in the pool. If you happened to get within a few feet of her it was like swimming in the sea at Blackpool with foamy white hairy stuff floating on the surface. Yuk. Still, at least you got the aroma of Lily of the Valley rather than Shit of the Sewage you used to get at Blackpool. She also used to wash her smalls in the sink in the changing rooms; when I say smalls though they were more like bigs. Had she been kind enough to donate a pair to the Red Cross they could have been used to house a small family of homeless people, and with the hair from her pits knit them Mo Hair jumpers to keep them warm too.

As well as nutty Mo there was also a bloke who I used to refer to as *James Herriot*. For anybody who missed this 1980s family viewing programme or hasn't read the books, James Herriot was a vet who spent his days dealing with the trials and tribulations of animal welfare in a farming community. This meant that he spent a considerable amount of time with his arm shoved armpit deep up the back end of a cow. Hence, when I say the man at the pool had brown arms only up to his biceps I think you will get my drift!

Anyway, after giving *Shamu* a run for his money by dragging the dinghy behind while I gurgled and sprayed water ungracefully out my mouth, I eventually managed to reach the oar, flinging it into the boat to cries of,

'Ouch, that hit my head'. At this point I realised I had another dilemma; did I try to get into the boat again? Hmm…If you've ever tried to get on a lilo in a pool, never mind get into a dinghy from the icy depths of a lake, you'll realise my problem. Granted lilos are a slightly more slippery adversary, as you get on one side only to slide off the other as the combination of sun cream and rubber result in a fight that looks like a scene from Jaws. So, the prospect of hauling my soggy arse up and over the side was not one I relished as it would no doubt result in the inflatable vessel depositing its current occupant into the arctic waters causing more abuse and bad language from Claire than I could possibly type.

The only alternative then, was that I would have to swim and drag the boat to the shore with Claire on board looking like the Queen of bloody Sheba. I was now feeling like I needed to be covered in goose fat from head to foot. No, this isn't a fantasy thing but it was getting mighty cold in there and a bit of lard smeared on me wouldn't have gone amiss. Still, at least we had the two oars now so Claire could help my painfully slow progress by rowing. Well, that's what you'd think. At this point I realised she had the co-ordination of a chimp on LSD as she kept bopping me on the head every time the oar came out the water. What a sight for sore eyes we must have made: one fully-clothed bedraggled blonde dragging a dinghy containing a manic-looking brunette who was making a worse attempt at rowing than the owl and the pussy cat put together… and neither of them have arms so how they managed to go out in the pea green boat God only knows.

We eventually made our way towards the jetties accompanied by sounds of, 'Ouch. Gurgle gurgle' and 'Oops…. Sooorry' played on repeat. It was harder than it looked, swimming whilst being assaulted by an oar, but the entertainment value for onlookers was immense.

Now you may recall that we had a couple of other friends on dry land. So, you may be lulled into thinking that they would be watching this debacle unfold with concern for our safety, ready to call on some burly bloke with a boat and bulging biceps to come and rescue us in our time of need. Oh no, our trusty mates had got bored of watching the rowing event of the year and so were now sunbathing on the grass like a couple of chameleons, unaware of our near-death experience. Okay, slight exaggeration but even so. It's only when I stood over them dripping cold water onto their sun-kissed skin that they notice my sodden state.

'Ahhhh…Bloody hell, that's cold. Oh…have you been for a swim?' asked Gill innocently. I will not write down my reply but it is fair to say that it was not one that could be aired before the 9 o'clock watershed.

6

In Retail Therapy

The Lake District has much to offer in the form of stunning views, gorgeous lakes, friendly people with warm and inviting pubs on a cold wet day. One thing it does not offer, however, is high-end fashion or designer outlets unless you count Berghaus as the new Burberry. I can't see Victoria Beckham turning up at a fashion show with the latest designer rucksack flung over her shoulder:

'And here we can see Victoria wearing a beautiful off the shoulder black Stella McCartney dress accessorised with an over the shoulder Freeflow 10L pink and black backpack.'

It's just not going to happen.

The shops are, however, great if you are looking for walking gear. I'm not a great shopper; it isn't something that I really enjoy unless you count shopping as: one shop then pub, another shop then another pub and so on and so forth. By the time you get home you think, *'What the hell did I buy those orange shoes for? Hmm...they won't even go with the lime green dress I bought last time.'* Pissed shopping. You should try it. Just make sure you keep the receipts.

Shopping for walking gear is easier as the choice is more limited, although just as expensive as some as your designer stuff; you could spend a small fortune kitting yourself out for a walk in the hills. You see people going out in all their expensive new gear looking like seasoned walkers, only to come back a few hours later looking slightly dejected that their expensive attire is now covered in mud, soaked through and smelling of cow shit. Still, it is very necessary to have the right gear if you don't want to end up looking a bit of a halfwit on that mountain rescue programme. I did actually once see a woman dressed up to the nines in high heels tottering her way up a dirt track; she looked more out of place than Jeremy Clarkson would've in a pink feathered boa stood at the helm of a float at Gay Pride week.

It makes me laugh when I see people wandering around Windermere in all the gear with walking sticks (the hiking ones not the aids for the elderly) looking like they are about to accompany Sir Edmund Hilary on an expedition to the peaks of the Himalayas, when in reality they are going to sit in Costa Coffee and have a stroll down to the lake. Don't get me wrong, this is a nice thing to do and I'm not knocking the people that do it, but do you really need two poles, a bar of Kendal Mint Cake and sturdy boots to get there?

Actually, to be fair, the poles could come in handy as Lake Windermere is home to a large number of swans, and they're really vicious buggers I can tell you. Whenever I come across one of the long-necked assassins I tend to give them a really wide berth; you get a chorus of hissing just for walking within ten feet of them. Oh, unless you have bread, then they will take your bloody hand off....and they can break your arm you know!

As is the norm, my shopping expeditions are never quite as straightforward as they should be; a simple purchase of a pair of walking sandals for example should be a breeze, right? Not where I'm concerned.

As I lack concentration these days, I find that as I wander round the shops my mind is not entirely on the task at hand. Thoughts of... *What shall I have for tea?* Or, *I wonder why older people wear socks with sandals?* and, *Why do they always feel they have to tell you how old they are?* pop inexplicably into my head.

It's true though you know, whenever you meet somebody over the age of 70 they quite often tell you how old they are. It's like they have Age Tourette's. The other thing that they feel obliged to do is tell you either about their health or their dead spouse. What is it about getting older that makes you think you can discuss your most intimate health issues with a complete stranger? And more importantly, think the stranger wants to know?

They should make a special *OAP Embarrassing Bodies* with some doddery old bloke happily discussing erectile dysfunction or their prostate and bladder problems, or a nice lady called Ethel talking about how she has a vaginal itch that she can only put down to the recent sexual encounter with Bert from Flat 3 in the warden accommodation she just moved into. No erectile problems there then…

Maybe it's just me they open up to, as I do tend to attract the older folk when I'm either at the shops or out walking. They always say I have a kind face and warm smile. Humph. They haven't seen me when I'm behind them when they stop randomly at the top of an escalator to check the contents of their shopping bag.

On one walk this year I met an elderly gentleman who was sat part way up a hill sheltering from a shower. Being the sociable kind I said,

'Morning… It's a bit of a miserable day to be out walking, isn't it?' to which he replied,

'Yes, it is but when you get to 81 you have to make the most of it.' Oh, here we go…Strike 1…that's the Age Tourette's out the way.

'Gosh! 81! And still coming up here. You must be very fit for your age?' A leading question I know.

'I've been coming up here for years, I enjoy the walking but I can't quite do as much as I used to. I have had two hip replacements you know?'…Strike 2…*No I didn't know as I have only just met you and unless you were stood there, stark bollock naked showing off your scars, I don't think it would be at the forefront of my mind.* OMG! WHAT a thought! A naked 81-year-old bloke roaming the hills of the Lake District with two poles, a rucksack, and a couple of other wrinkly sacks on display. I bet that photo wouldn't make it to the final of the *Countryfile* calendar. Of course, I don't say this, instead I opt for,

'Blimey, it's amazing these days isn't it, I bet they've given you a new lease of life, haven't they?' This is his chance to now tell me all about what he can still do.

'Oh yes, it's just a shame my Dorothy isn't here to enjoy it with me. We'd come up here every year at this time for a week, that's until she became too poorly. I lost her last year.' Strike 3 and OUT!

I always think that is an odd phrase to use 'I lost someone', it makes it sound like you put them somewhere and for the life of you, you just can't remember where.

Anyway, back to the sandal shopping. On this particular day, I was in a very distracted mood, so as I aimlessly traipsed around one of the many walking shops that Ambleside has to offer, looking at everything but sandals. I was therefore only vaguely aware of what was going on around me. As I looked at the packets of revolting dried food the camping cuisine section had on display, I noticed that there was a sleeping bag strewn across the floor. I thought nothing further of it until it suddenly lurched towards me and shot bolt upright like a giant purple worm on Viagra.

'AAAHHH!!!' I screamed, jumping backwards with a panther-like reaction that James Bond would have been proud of. Unfortunately, unlike James Bond who is smooth, suave and sophisticated, I'm clumsy, inept and accident prone, and as I pirouetted backwards I knocked the neat display of drinking containers that were just behind me, sending them crashing to the floor. At the sound of my high-pitched squeal, accompanied by the percussion section of clanging flasks, a man promptly popped his head out from the sleeping bag looking like the proverbial rabbit caught in headlights.

'I am so sorry,' he muttered, 'I was just trying it out for size to see if I could fit in it with the top fastened.' What sort of simpleton lies in a sleeping bag in the middle of a shop testing it out for size for God sake? Oh, I know … a six-foot irresponsible goon with a love of scaring the crap out of unsuspecting passers-by.

Being the non-confrontational sort though I said,

'Oh, it's okay… you gave me a bit of a scare that's all, I wasn't expecting it to move.'

I would have been less scared if old Berty Bollocks from Flat 3 had appeared waggling his thrush-infected todger in my direction with nothing on but his socks and sandals. I was convinced for at least a month afterwards that I would be on some TV programme where they assault unsuspecting shoppers in a veiled attempt at comedy. *Game for a Laugh?* Not likely!

Unfortunately, my shopping nightmare didn't end there as I continued with slightly damp undergarments, but more focused this time, in the pursuit of the comfy walking sandal. The next shop had no sleeping bags, tents or any other such paraphernalia that could contain a hiding six-foot hairy imbecile, so I perused the footwear with the determination of a woman on a mission. I found a pair that were in the right price bracket (cheap) that I thought would do nicely.

It was the sort of shop where all the shoes are in boxes stacked like a game of Shoe Jenga. This involves having to search through the stacks to find your size and style, then inevitably have to manoeuvre the box from the bottom without disrupting the whole pile. I found the ones I wanted relatively easily though, so removed my walking boots and socks to try them on.

It may be worth mentioning at this point that the reason I wanted some sandals was that I had just finished a long walk, so my feet had been sweating profusely, and now had the pungent aroma of cellophane wrapped Blue Stilton that had been left in a steamer for ten hours. Having put the sandals on and traipsed up and down the shop to test for comfort, I decided that although cheap and aesthetically pleasing, they were about as comfortable as having sandpaper fixed to your feet with a bit of chicken wire.

The sandals were fastened with clasps that were secured by clicking the two ends into place; granted, a nifty and quick way to fasten anything. Unfortunately, in the case of these sandals it was a bit too secure as I struggled to separate the two ends getting more and more frantic as time went on. I had flashbacks to the time I was stuck in a £300 dress in John Lewis that ended with the assistant ripping the netting that I'd caught in the zip. Surely lightning couldn't strike twice as they say?

Seeing my face redden with embarrassment, or

exertion, the assistant came over to ask if he could help. At this point I had to admit defeat and explain that I couldn't get the bloody thing off my foot.

'Don't worry, they are a bit fiddly sometimes,' he said nonchalantly, 'Let me help you.' At this point he swooped down to the aid of what he perceived to be a damsel in distress but was soon recoiling at the cheesy whiff that assaulted his nostrils. As he fiddled with the clasp, I could see he was fighting the urge to run for the Scholl foot spray and antibacterial hand-wash.

As he twiddled, pulled and tugged at the offending sandal, the clasp remained firmly in place and his frustration deepened to the point where a very unsightly vein started to throb quite profusely in his forehead. At this point I was sweating like a pig in a polo neck and my face was flushed with embarrassment, as other shoppers stared in a mixture of amusement and a *'Thank God it isn't me'* look. The assistant had also now admitted defeat, or had been overcome by the fumes of the Feta feet, and had called on another sales assistant to help in this *Krypton Factor*-like challenge.

We struggled on for a further ten minutes pulling and pushing the offending clasp to try and release its grasp from my intensely smelly foot but unfortunately, it was holding on tighter than a vertigo sufferer at a bungee jump.

Eventually one of my fellow shoppers suggested spraying WD40 on it; well if nothing else it would improve the smell. So off tootled Giles in search of some. Yes, I'd been there that long, I was now on first name terms with him and half the shop, as well as being privy to half his life story. When a bloke has been sniffing the overpowering odours of your smelly feet for the past 20 minutes you have to occupy his mind somehow to stop him from keeling over.

The WD40 arrived and was sprayed on the clasp; the crowd waited with baited breath. Oh, okay, Marge and Fred, who'd been watching the whole thing while munching on Kendal Mint Cake, let out a combined, 'Ooohhhh'.

After a couple of anxious seconds while we let it penetrate, Giles began to fumble with the clasp wiggling it back and forth to lubricate it.

At this point, being a horny mare, I had visions of a different sort of fumbling and lubrication but, I realised he must've thought I had feet to rival the Gruyere production company, I doubted whether he would be interested. This amply demonstrated my state of mind. It's a poor state of affairs when you get turned on by a shop assistant with a prominent vein and hair that looked like it last saw shampoo when he left school, just because he's playing with your foot.

With a few more twists the clasp eventually came free and the sandal was off accompanied by shouts of, 'Yeah!!' from Marge and Fred.

It was with a big grin that Giles turned to me and said, 'You'll not be wanting to buy these then?' Oh how I laughed...

7

Virgin on the Ridiculous

Like a lot of women these days I've always worked full time in order to be able to afford the lifestyle that I have. This involved balancing family life and work with the dexterity of a juggler spinning very large plates.

Since leaving college as a quiet and unconfident 18-year-old, I've worked for the same large company but, I have to say, it's hardly recognisable from the business I joined in 1986. For a start, you used to be able to smoke in the office. Imagine that now! I used to sit next to a woman who smoked like a factory chimney with a fag in her mouth and one burning in the ashtray. This resulted in her having the sort of phlegmy cough that sounded like you could use it to stick up wallpaper. Being a non-smoker I used to have to go home and shower immediately so that I didn't smell like I was wearing Eau de Fag Ash when I went out. Then there were the Friday lunchtime drinks: two hours in the pub then back to work for an hour before going off out again for Happy Hour. Ahhh those were the days.

As the decades have gone by and attitudes have changed, the Friday lunchtime sessions and afternoons of high jinks are no more but, being a large company, there are still a number of us left from those halcyon days. As it approaches somebody's big birthday, dodgy photographs will appear that have been safely hidden in the archives with somebody's much forgotten Duran Duran LP and lycra leotard.

Blimey, there have been some unquestionably awful haircuts and fashions over the years, the worst of which has to be the 1980s when perms, blonde streaks and mullet cuts were the height of fashion.

Looking back at photos of myself in those days I look like a Bananarama reject with a frizzy blonde perm, leggings that made me look like a chunky Max Wall and beads big enough to go ten-pin bowling with. This was then replaced by the Dallas look, with the permed hair getting bigger along with the shoulder pads. Had I turned too quickly in a confined space, I'd have had some poor unsuspecting sod whipped onto their backside quicker than Pam Ewing could say, 'Bobby, stop day dreaming and get out of that shower.'

The only consolation is that I was not alone in my fashion blunders as the photos doing the rounds at the office prove. I'm sure that I look better today, although do we all say that? Mind you, as I get ever nearer the Big Five Oh and somebody brings out a recent photo of a night out, I may wonder why I ever wore a lime green dress and orange shoes.

The only other problem with there being so many women of fuzzy thinking age in one office, is that we are all suffering from the same menopausal mood swings and hot flushes. All you hear all day are fans going on and off, or somebody crying because her pen ran out and she's not sure why she's crying but it was a very nice pen. Okay, that may be ever such a slight exaggeration but you get my drift. I have to say poor old Michael Fish could no more predict our moods than he did the storms of 1987.

My job these days occasionally requires me to travel and, as with my little jaunt to Glasgow demonstrated, driving usually ends up with me getting more lost than a dog-less David Blunkett, so I decided that it would be a better option to travel more by train. Up to now, I've always managed to get the right one, although I did have one close call when I was sat on a train sipping my coffee and munching my Danish staring at fellow passengers walking past the window and noting how quiet the train was. I remember thinking, *I'm sure we should have left the station by now* ...only to find out that it was actually the train in front I should have got and this one wasn't leaving any time soon. It never twigged that I was on the wrong one.

I'm sure the bored British Rail bods do this to catch out befuddled travellers. They undoubtedly sit at the track side, watching with amusement as it dawns on the poor sods that they are on the wrong train and then have to quickly gather up all their stuff in a vain attempt to catch the one they should be on without looking like some demented bag lady. Still there was no harm done on that occasion, I didn't end up in Bridlington instead of Bournemouth.

For a short time last winter, I worked in Wolverhampton for two to three days a week, so a regular commute from Manchester was required. As I inevitably spent a large amount of time doing a very poor impression of Michael Flatly on the platform in an attempt to keep warm, I decided I really needed to invest in a lovely warm coat. As the cold mornings kicked in, this became essential if I wasn't to lose a limb or one of my other extremities to frostbite. What I failed to think about at the time of the purchase however, was the colour. Did I go for a versatile black one? Did I go for a nice pale cream one? No. In my infinite wisdom, I went for a lovely pillar box red one.

Now, you may be thinking 'What's wrong with that? Red is a nice colour.' But when you think about *where* I intended to wear it, it turned out to be a huge mistake. Every sodding day I got approached by fellow commuters asking my advice about departure times, what facilities were aboard the trains, the rules for the transportation of live animals, whether I could help load grandma's mobility scooter onto the train and unbelievably, in one instance, an enquiry about if they needed their passport to go to Scotland! Yes! People thought I was a Virgin train employee!

It got to the point where I just used to either look at the board for the times or make something up that sounded plausible. I once told a particularly obnoxious bloke who clicked his fingers at me to get my attention that the first-class section of the train to Euston was now at the rear, making him scuttle off in haste to the other end of the platform only to find out that when his train got in he was at the wrong end. Pompous arse... Served him right.

Despite being approached at the train station more times than a hairdressing prostitute offering a Clit and Blow, the coat was lovely and warm and it did prevent me freezing my backside off daily so I continued to wear it. Well it had cost a fortune and warmth wins over frivolous spending any day.

Anyway, as I am now a seasoned rail commuter having travelled the length and breadth of the country on more journeys than Michael Portillo can shake a stick at, I thought I would impart some of my experience when picking where you want to sit.

Never sit next to the irritating ignoramus, in his sharp suit, who talks loudly on his phone so that people can hear his Business Conversations, and who thinks he's the next winner of *The Apprentice*. Even 30 minutes of this is too much as he comes out with phrases like, 'Okay dudes, let's throw that out there to roll around the table and gather ideas' or, 'Awesome... Let's run with it and see where we end up'. Oh, and a personal favourite of mine; 'The idea has been germinating in my mind for a while but I just wanted to implant it so it can grow.' What an utter tosser.

You may also want to dodge the bloke in the anorak with the thermos flask, Tupperware container and a copy of *Famous Railway Journeys*. He will undoubtedly engage you in a conversation about the train journeys he's been on, boring you rigid while you nod and smile politely like a mute wobbly headed Cheshire cat. He will then proceed to open up the airtight container to reveal the pungent egg butties his mother prepared for him that morning. Anybody passing will now think that either you, or him, has tremendous wind as the fragrance of eggy flatulence wafts around the compartment.

If there's a woman sat at a table with humongous breasts don't sit opposite. You will spend the entire journey trying to avoid looking at them as they rest wobbling on the table like a couple of very large blancmanges on a tray, whilst comparing each one to the size of your head and wondering, if she was to wear a Wonderbra would she look like she had two small bald children nestling down her front?

I must confess that I find train journeys dull and tiring at the best of times. However, I'll always resist the urge to stimulate my brain with an on-board coffee that tastes like left-over fag ash, opting instead for music or a good book to while away the hours. I tend to avoid too many fluids to be honest though, unless it's wine of course, as I hate having to pay a visit to the swaying conveniences. Although I know that I've pressed the button to lock the door, I must check it ten times… just in case. Despite the signs, I'm always surprised by how many people don't though. You go to what you think is an empty lavatory only for the doors to slide back revealing Derek the train buff with his pants round his ankles now reading the *Fly Fishing Monthly*. Ahhhhhh... So it wasn't the egg butties after all!

If like me you don't like using the loos on the train, then another word of warning is to also avoid the poky public conveniences at small railway stations. These should only be used in desperate situations. You're okay with the ones where the robbing gits charge you a small fortune to relieve yourself, as the attendant makes sure you keep them clean. Woe betide anybody who splashes water or soap inappropriately. You'll be on the receiving end of a look that could wither an oak tree.

I had a particularly nasty experience in one of the unmanned toilets. On this occasion, I was in fact desperate after a long journey where the loos on the train were out of order; some bright spark had decided to jam it with enough toilet paper to decorate the local church hall for the Andrex puppy parade. Having taken a deep breath to get me over the stomach churning fumes filling the air, I headed for the first cubical available. Holy Crap! I was met with the sight of the biggest poo I had ever seen lurking menacingly at the bottom of the bowl like a brown toilet monster.

The other toilet was out of order so I had no choice but to use this one as I really needed to go. There was only one thing for it, I decided I needed to first flush the offending log before I parked my backside on the seat above it. This was a BIG mistake. As the water flooded into the toilet the stubborn bugger did not descend into the safety of the U-bend as predicted. Obviously his much bigger mate was blocking the way out to the freedom of the sewers. I watched in horror as the toilet rapidly filled with water and the newly released poo started to rise to the surface at great speed. It was like watching *Hunt for Red October* as the submarine-like faeces floated to the top. For the love of God. I wanted to shout 'Dive! Dive!' but with the steely determination of a poo on a mission to free itself from the confines of the toilet bowl it continued its ascent. What could I do other than rapidly make my escape before it landed at my feet like a big brown smelly gift from the gods!! I'm ashamed to say I didn't even go and tell anybody about the escaped poo for fear that they may think that it was mine; and the worse thing was, I still needed the loo!

Going back to the red coat though, I have to say the train station was not the only time that there was a case of mistaken identity while I was wearing the troublesome garment.

My friend Gill and I had been invited to a party in the depths of the Yorkshire Dales where any unfamiliar folk were eyed up with more suspicion than a priest in a synagogue. We arrived to check in at the only hotel available and, guessing by the judgemental expression on the receptionist's face, she assumed one of two things: either we were there to pull the local talent for a spot of 'Eee by gum' in the wee small hours or we'd be having rampant lesbian sex to the sounds of K.D Lang all night long. On this premise, she had decided the best thing to do was to give us a room that was located in an annex at the back of the hotel. The room, which opened directly onto the car park, was as far removed from the main reception as you could get, just in case the sounds of murmured pleasure were heard reverberating through the main hotel. Now that would never do!

Once we had checked in, Gill trundled off back to the car to get the extra bags she'd packed ...just in case. This girl does not believe in travelling light, packing more than Joan Collins and the whole of her entourage. As she rummaged in her car for the fourth pair of strappy shoes that, in the windswept and icy depths of the Dales, she was *never* going to wear - not even in a month of Sundays - I stood holding the door to our room waiting patiently but still wearing my coat to keep out the chilly wind that was whipping around my nether regions.

As it happened, another couple, having just arrived at the hotel car park started to walk towards me. *Oh!* I thought, *perhaps they want to ask where the hotel entrance is.* As they got nearer I put on my friendly face and a big smile to offer directions to the reception area, but on getting to me they just smiled back and said, 'Hi' and then walked right past me and into my room. *What the Fu...!!*

I didn't quite know what to say as I turned around slightly dumbstruck to see two dazed people looking round like they had just walked out of Narnia and into the wardrobe.

'Sorry..' the highly embarrassed man says, '..we thought that this was the hotel entrance with you stood there with the door open'.

The cheek! He thought I was the concierge! I wouldn't mind but since when do rural three star hotels have people on the door waiting to greet you with a smile and a willingness to carry your fake Louis Vuitton luggage for you?

Once the couple had made their hasty escape with faces redder than my coat, I dissolved into hysterical laughter at the ridiculousness of what had just happened. When Gill came back with more bags than Manchester Airport's left luggage department, she found me crumpled on the bed laughing like an asthmatic yak,

'What the hell's up with you?' she muttered from behind her vanity case. It took me a good ten minutes to calm down enough to tell her in a Norman Wisdom-like manner what had just happened. Fortunately, we didn't see the couple again during our stay and I no longer wear the red coat at hotels or railway stations.

8

Fuzzy Navels and Fuzzy Heads

I've made lots of really good friends over the years at work, and even though some have managed to escape and move on to different careers, we've stayed in touch, and whenever possible we go out to reminisce about the good old days and gossip about who's doing what.

I've also still got two of my closest and best friends from school, Emma and Gill, whom I love dearly and couldn't do without. Over the 35 years we've known each other, we've been on countless drunken nights out and had numerous holidays and weekends away and, although Emma has buggered off to a lovely sunnier life in Australia, we continue to have a great friendship that I'm sure will last a lifetime.

It was from one of these many nights out that we gave our girly get-togethers a name…. A Fuzzy Navel Night. For any of you who don't know, a Fuzzy Navel is a cocktail of peach schnapps and orange juice. They aren't the most potent of cocktails. In fact, it just feels like you're drinking orange juice, well unless I'm doing my best Tom Cruise impression and making them. Then the ratio of peach schnapps to orange is a little more weighted in favour of alcohol to fruit juice.

If you want the more potent variety, you can also add vodka to give you a Hairy Navel. Hmmm…. maybe not the most exotic name for a cocktail I'll admit. It doesn't exactly conjure up images of sipping from an elegant glass watching the sun set over a gorgeous sandy beach. No. A Hairy Navel depicts slurping alcohol from some fat hairy bloke's belly button along with months of fluff that's accumulated deep within the folds of his sticky gut. Yuk!! Mind you, having watched the film about the infamous Cynthia Payne, I bet you could find some blokes who'd pay good money to let you do that.

It's truly amazing the things some men find a turn on. I'm not exactly a prude, but for goodness sake how can watching somebody poo or have a golden shower be wank bank material? Performing your bodily functions is not exactly the sexiest thing in the world, but to have somebody wanting to watch you do it in front or, even more bizarrely, on them, is just wrong on so many levels! It's the multi-storey of wrongness.

And then there's the men who like to be dominated and treated like a slave. I've often thought that this could be quite useful to get your house cleaned for free as you sit there barking the occasional, 'You're a BAD BAD boy. Get on your hands and knees and scrub that floor or I'll have to come over there and punish you.' Although I'm not sure I want some perverted bloke in Marigolds ejaculating his man gunge all over my skirting boards when I order him to make sure he gets right into the corners.

I digress. Back to me and my pals. It was on one of these nights, when we were young and drinking homemade Fuzzy Navels, that resulted in me being the most inebriated, and ultimately most ill, that I've ever been.

It all started so well at Emma's house, the usual meeting point for a night out as she lived with her thoroughly modern Mum who, on nine times out of ten, was also out gallivanting. She never used to mind us girls starting our nights there with a few drinks, loud music and enough hair spray and make-up to put on a production at the local amateur dramatics. It also helped too that Emma's elderly neighbour was as deaf as a post as we used to have the latest hits blaring out of the stereo prior to our departure. This usually varied from U2 and Swing out Sister to Dick a Dum Dum by God knows who…. Yes, when pissed, Top of the Tots from the 1970s always made a guest appearance to much drunken hilarity. It did take some explaining however, when one night we blew the speakers, something about tweeters and woofers. I always thought that they were the cat and dog in *Tom and Jerry*. Apparently not.

As we were young and usually broke, we got the number 50 bus into Manchester for our night out. The journey in itself should have warned us that the little harmless Fuzzy Navels had lulled us into a false sense of security, what with it just being made of orange juice with a small kick, but actually they had packed more punch than *Rocky* in the movies I, II and III put together. As we reached the Apollo Theatre (yes, I think every town has one) Emma started to look a worrying shade of grey.

'Are you okay Em?' I slurred.

'Yeah, I just feel a bit ...' As she started to respond, what can only be described as a flood of luminous orange vomit spewed from her mouth, rivalled only by an eruption from Mount Vesuvius. As the bus driver braked heavier than Lewis Hamilton on a hairpin bend, the river of projectile puke flowed down the centre of the bus letting nothing get in its way. People gasped in horror as the lava like fluid enveloped their bags in its wake and cries of,

'What the fuck?' could be heard throughout the bus as it made its way down the aisle.

You can imagine then that we were about as popular as Margaret Thatcher at a coal miners' reunion. Needless to say, we were unceremoniously thrown off the bus about a mile from the city centre.

Whilst Emma carried on erupting into the nearest bush, Gill and I discussed what we should do next. Anybody listening would have thought we were conversing in some strange Swahili tongue but we understood each other perfectly.

'Wot sssshall we do now?' I incoherently asked.
'Dunno, I feel ssshlober. I don't know 'bout youse, but I shthink we best take Em home. Ssssheees pished as a

fart. Did sssshhee drunk more than ush?'

So, after the pished bussssh ride back we then completed our short walk to her house. This took a disproportionate amount of time due to the fact that we were supporting the vomit queen and swaying and meandering off course more than a fishing boat in a force nine gale. We vaguely considered stopping at a local pub for a swift nightcap, but as Em now smelt like a bucket of year old cottage cheese, and looked like a Jackson Pollock painting, we decided to call it a night.

9

Plethora of Pillocks

Unfortunately, with age we don't seem to learn from our youthful drinking antics, no matter how bad the hangover the next day. Gone are the painful memories of the African steel band playing rhythmically in your brain, and you can no longer recall the sensation that somehow you woke with yesterday's gym socks in your mouth.

As ever, with the consumption of alcohol, what little common sense I possessed packs its bags, waves goodbye and buggers off to find somewhere to hide until sobriety returns. You know that whilst you're drinking, the little voice inside your head is saying, *'Oh for Goodness sake! Not again! Do you not remember the last time?'* but this can be easily ignored as you sip on a nice glass of *Pinot Grigio*.

Since becoming single again my Fuzzy Navel nights out took on a slightly different twist with friends making it their mission to find me a date whether I wanted one or not. Well, when they say date, what they really mean is sex. Phrases like, 'You need to get back on the horse' and, 'Give Vernon a rest for God sake and get a proper man' were frequently bandied about. How good do they make me feel? I'm like a cross between Frankie Dettori and the Duracell bunny.

They were not entirely wrong though as, feeling as frisky as a teenage boy in a porn shop, I really did need a good *'seeing to'* as my eloquent friends would say. However, I wasn't going to just jump into bed with any Tom, Dick or Harry, whoever they were, or even all three. I do have standards, so the task of finding me a suitable man that I actually liked, turned out to be more difficult than locating the Holy Grail.

I don't crack mirrors when I check my reflection, and people tell me I don't look my age, so you would think I was in with a chance. There again, I'm not sure how they can tell that I have a youthful demeanour. It's not like I have Age Tourette's and instantly start the sentence with, 'I'm 46 you know'. Still, I will take it as a compliment and run with it, as the tosser on the train would say.

So that you can make your own mind up, whether I was justified in turning down all advances in favour of a night in with a glass of wine and Vernon, I will introduce you to just a few of the dingbats I've pulled during my barren time as a single woman in her mid-forties. Some of them never even got to tell me their names, so I've created ones that I felt accurately reflected their personality.

First I met Cheesy Charlie; a particular corny chap who strolled over whilst I was having a quiet scoop or two in lovely Marple Bridge with Claire. We were sat chatting, catching up on what had been going on in our lives since we last met. This is always entertaining as Claire is very much like me, being accident prone and a bit of a dimwit.

To give you an example; one Christmas we were meeting at Piccadilly station in Manchester for an afternoon out. I arrived at the designated time at the agreed location: by the big Christmas tree: I thought Claire must have been running late until I got the text saying,

'I'm here, where are you?' Odd, I thought, but replied,

'I'm here. By the big Christmas tree. Where are you?'

Reply: 'I'm by the big Christmas tree, I can't see you'

Reply: 'Are you at Piccadilly you dozy mare?

Reply: 'Yes, cheeky! By the departures board. By that huge frigging tree covered in baubles'

Reply: 'You can't be there, unless you are playing hide and seek with the elves looking for Santa's sack.'

Having enough of the banter and fearing Christmas could have come and gone, I rang…. It turned out we were both at the station *and* by the Christmas tree…. Just opposite sides of it! As our vision was obscure by the spectacularly baubled foliage, we couldn't see each other and as I kept walking round it, so did she. It never occurred to either of us to say, 'Stay where you are'. We must have looked like a right couple of numb nuts circling round like a pair of tree sharks. Three times we went around on the hunt for each other. Yes, I know. Unbelievable!

Anyway, on this particular night Claire had come out looking a bit like something out of a Scorsese movie having dyed her hair red instead of the warming auburn it was supposed to be. She'd picked up the wrong box and didn't wonder why the sink looked like a butcher's bin when she was doing it. All thoughts of pulling were therefore not even within a mile of my thought process.

As we sat there minding our own business, safely stowed away in the corner so nobody would mistake her for a Janet Street-Porter fan, along sauntered a cocky bloke with the novel chat up line of,

'Ooh, you two look just like strawberries and cream and I'm sure you are just as sweet. Can I buy you two gorgeous ladies a drink?' REALLY? Is he for real or had I just been transported into some bad 70s porn movie (not that I have seen one I'll have you know). I had visions of him opening his shirt to reveal a medallion and a small poodle pinned to his chest.

For once both Claire and I were stunned into silence. Well what could you say in response to that? I tried to think back to the days when *Blind Date* was the must-see Saturday night viewing, but they would have said something along the lines of, 'You can lick this cream off any time and then you can be my strawberry fool', What a God-awful programme that was, full of innuendos and corny chat up lines when all they really wanted wasn't love, but a free weekend away. As we were not on *Blind Date* and I in no way wanted licking off by this wannabe Lothario, I just said,

'Erm... no thanks, we're fine thank you.' See... a nice, polite response like my mother taught me. He then gave us what was supposed to be a dazzling smile but looked more like trapped wind and said,

'As you're the best-looking women in the pub I wondered if me and my mate could join you?' Again, I'm very polite and say, 'We haven't seen each other for ages so we just really want to have a quiet drink and a chat thanks.' That had to work, didn't it?

'Oh, come on. You don't want to be sat here on your own all night, two beautiful young girls like you.' *Erm. Yes, we do.*

Unfortunately, it seemed that subtle polite rebuffs were not going to get rid of this clichéd Casanova. I'm not even sure he would've got the message if a big sign hit him squarely in the face saying, 'Piss off! They're not interested pal!' Claire took over at this point and said,

'Look mate, we're not interested. Now if you don't mind I'm just in the middle of telling my friend here all about my new job at the STD clinic.'

He sort of did that half laugh half huff that people do when they're not sure if you are joking or not, but then on seeing our serious faces he turned sharply on his heels making a swift beeline for the safety of his friend. I'm still not sure if he was worried if Claire would see him there or if the concern was catching something from sitting at the same table. Of course, it was total codswallop as she has no such job, but it always gets rid of them saying you work at the clap clinic.

Then there was Bog Breath Brendan. Now I'm not overly fussy about a man being suited and booted all the time, but what I really don't like is a lack of personal hygiene. When a man's hands look like they've been used to tunnel his way out of an underground cave and then left for two weeks for the dirt to become engrained in the skin so Swarfega and an electric sander would be needed to remove it. Or when his breath could drop a skunk at 40 paces. Then I have to say, this is an immediate turn off. I could've consumed two whole bottles of wine and they could look like Brad Pitt and I still wouldn't go within breathing distance of them.

I was out with work colleagues one night, and we were in a particularly noisy pub in Manchester, where the only way you could hear what was being said to you was to get up close and personal. Unfortunately for me I attracted the attention of Britain's answer to the energy crisis. You know how cow dung can be used to power thermal energy? Well this bloke's breath could sustain a small town on the methane being emitted when he spoke.

When he asked me if I would like a drink I was tempted to order a glass of *Pinot Grigio* for me and a pint of Listerine for him, but I politely declined saying I was in a round with my friends. He then went on to tell me that his name was Brendan and he was a landscape gardener. Ahhh… that explained the dirty hands.

As he continued to breathe stale cabbage into my face whilst he hung onto his pint pot with his mucky mitts, all I could think about was his bad hygiene. It seemed that he had swerved most of these daily simple, but essential ablutions, for some time. As I hastily made my escape to the toilets to check that my make-up hadn't been stripped from my face by the fumes, Brendan gave me his number hoping that I would lose all sense of smell and call him. Needless to say, I didn't. That landscape horticulturist was never going to be doing any bedding in anywhere near my lady garden…

Another favourite of mine was Rat-Arsed Romeo. When my friends and I first started frequenting the local watering holes in the hope of getting inebriated on two halves of Woodpecker, we used to go out in Didsbury. As well as being local, it was packed with pubs and more importantly packed with pubs where you could get served even if you were under the legal drinking age. In fact, some nights it had more sixth form students in the bars than you got at some of the lectures. The smell of Paco Rabanne mixed with Clearasil wafted at you as the boys stood huddled in the corner, having sent the tallest and oldest looking one to the bar to get the drinks.

Meanwhile, the girls used to plaster on more make-up than the Joker and stagger around in heels so high we could have performed at the circus. Just as a precaution, I used to take my sister Katy's driving licence with me; it wasn't like it is these days where it's easier to get a bacon butty in a synagogue than it is to get a drink in a pub when you're underage.

When deciding where to go on a night out with best friend Gill, we thought it would be a good idea to relive our 80s youth and try a night out in Didsbury again, although this time less make-up was required and my hair didn't look like an electrocuted poodle in a wind tunnel. Unfortunately, on the night we chose to go, there had been a one-day cricket match at Old Trafford so the pubs were filled with drunken blokes talking about googlies and leg overs or something like that anyway, maybe I have added the word *leg* in there!

Now we all know that when groups of men and women, get together for an all-day session, the result is not pretty and this was no exception. It had been a warm day so where shorts, flip-flops, sunglasses and a tight flowery shirt spray painted onto his six pack, may have been acceptable for the cricket, it did not look so good in a trendy bar at night. However, the bloke wearing them, having consumed his body weight in beer throughout the day, thought that he was God's gift to women. He was all swathed in *Look at me. I'm gorgeous wrapping paper.*

As he flip-flopped towards me looking a bit like a pissed penguin with the fashion sense of… well a penguin probably (they aren't known for being natty dressers now are they?) he slurred the following innovative chat up line, 'Hello gorgeous, has anybody told you that you have beautiful eyes?' Good God. It must have taken him an age to come up with that classic.

I was actually quite surprised he could see my eyes or my face, through the haze of alcohol and the reflection from his teeth. Unlike Bog Breath Brendan, this fella had dentistry that looked like he cleaned them in bleach. I felt like taking his sunglasses off his head and wearing them to stop the glare. This was not the end of his chat up repertoire however, as before I could say a word he followed this up with, 'And you have a fantastic arse. God I would love to take you home and fuck your brains out.' Yes! You read that right… *Fuck your brains out*. I was slightly stunned for a moment as I stared at this complete moron in astonishment. You know when I said I was horny? Well at that very moment thoughts of sex would have come further down my list of things to do than stick pins in my eyes and listen to *The Birdy Song* on repeat for 24 hours non-stop.

What does a girl say in such a situation? Should I try the, *'That would be very nice but I've just come out of prison and I have to be home by ten or my parole will be revoked'?*….No, he may offer to 'fuck my brains out' at my place. Or maybe, *'Unfortunately you are not my type, I prefer women and my partner and I are very happy together'*…. Oh no that would never work. He would want to watch, then 'fuck both our brains out'!! I could go for the less polite, *'Sod off Romeo, I wouldn't entertain you if you were the last man on earth and the future of the human race depended on it.'*…

Now, while this is the truth, it's not in my nature to be aggressive and besides, I wouldn't recommend it when the Romeo in question had been on the beer all day. Although, it would have been quite entertaining to watch him try to run after me in those flip-flops. So instead, as we picked up our bags to leave, I went for the sarcastic approach that was totally wasted on him,

'Gosh what charming and lovely compliments, and such a romantic offer. Unfortunately, we are just off now and my husband is picking us up outside, but I hope you find somebody with very little brains so that when you fuck them out it's not much of a loss.'

Then there was Old Boy Roy. Now, as I've mentioned I do attract the older chap, usually when I'm out walking the hills. On this occasion though, I outdid myself as I pulled an elderly gent in a pub. I do tend to be a little too polite sometimes and I never really like to tell somebody that their attentions are not really required, especially when they look like it's their only night out of the home and next week it will be back to Bingo and Scrabble tournaments with Ethel and Mable.

On one of Emma's trips back to the UK we'd gone up to the Lakes for a couple of relaxing days and to talk our way round the fells and the pubs. On this occasion, we were sat in a really nice watering hole in Bowness-on-Windermere that's very popular with locals and tourists alike. The only thing that puts me off it, are the stuffed animals that are located around the place. It's a bit disconcerting drinking your half of Dizzy Blonde with a moth-eaten weasel staring at you like he's pleading with you to save him from having to watch yet another bunch of well-oiled men on stag nights singing *Mr Brightside*. Yes, believe it or not, the Lake District does attract groups of lads celebrating the impending nuptials of one of the gang. I always find it a bit strange that they would choose the Lakes, as it isn't exactly Party Central with Bowness offering only a couple of clubs for late night drinking.

I use the word clubs loosely. One of them is actually the downstairs of a pub where you have to pay for the privilege of dancing in the claustrophobic cellar whilst being surreptitiously groped by some passing half-cut imbecile swaying more than a palm tree in high wind... Am I selling it to you? If you just want to have a late-night boogie and you don't mind the smell of stale sweat as some bloke wafts his arms in the air to Avicii like he's at a festival, then you may find it okay.

The other place is slightly bigger, but on the one night I've ventured there, the clientele consisted of me with three friends and a couple of homeless people each nursing a half pint so they could stay out of the cold. Still, as you didn't have to peel your feet off the carpet every time you took a step, I consider it to be a classier establishment.

On Em's visit this time though, we were not out for clubbing, we were just having a few quiet drinks and a meal, well that was the plan. The pub was busy as usual, so when a couple of older blokes asked if they could sit on the two vacant stools at our table we couldn't exactly say, '*No, stay standing. It will do your arthritis the world of good...*'

As they sat down they started to chat to us, first of all getting the Age Tourette's out of the way by telling us they were both 78 (Strike One!) and were having their monthly night out together. Bless, they had been friends for years and always met up to have a few beers and a chat. They lived locally so the conversation moved on to walks in the area and then ultimately golf. Emma is a keen golfer, having taken it up later in life, so was eager to listen to Alan recount all his golfing tales about holes in one and how to get out of a bunker. I, on the other hand am not, so this left me talking to Roy about his children, grandchildren and pet Border Collie named Pat after his dead wife (Strike Two!) Yeah, you've got it: 'Pat the dog'.

They were actually quite good company so we stayed for another drink and then another. There are advantages to chatting to older men: they usually have interesting stories to tell, they don't have egos the size of the Grand Canyon and you don't feel that they are trying to get in your knickers for a game of hide the shrunken sausage. Well, that is until Roy politely asked if we wanted to go back to his for a coffee and then turned around to Alan and whispered a bit on the loud side to compensate for the loss of hearing, 'I told you I should have washed my sheets today'. EEEWWW!!

I don't care if he was joking, I now had visions of

him stripping off to reveal a body that looked like it had been on a hot wash for too long, whilst I lay on his stained sheets waiting for the Viagra to kick in. This was not a nice image to end the night on and totally put me off any thoughts I had of eating. We returned alone to the caravan to drink ourselves into a stupor with Absolut vodka in the vain hope of obliterating this image from our minds forever…. It didn't work.

So, as you can see from this merry band of gentlemen, at this point in my life the prospect of a night out with any of them would have been about as much fun as getting a head cold.

What is it they say? There's somebody for everybody. Hmm… maybe my somebody just happened to be battery operated.

10

Nudge Nudge, Wink Wink!

Before I move on from telling you about some of the charming and wonderful men who have entered into my life ever so briefly, I must tell you about my most ardent admirer. This delightful fella was one of my neighbours and, for reasons that will become apparent, I've named him 'Winky Man'.

Part way through the summer, the young couple who lived at the rear of my property, moved out after deciding it was time to buy a house. I like to think it was nothing to do with me, after all, I didn't trump like a pot-bellied pig on a daily diet of sprouts and beans, and I hadn't brought any men back to romp the night away either. All other noises could be easily disguised by playing Smooth FM at low volume, so I wasn't too worried about that either. The couple had been really quiet too, especially considering there were two people living there, so I was a bit concerned as to who would move in: a person with a love of playing Metallica at full volume or worse still, a person with a love of playing

Barry Manilow at full volume into the wee small hours?

So, when the new tenant moved in I was quite pleased that, although I hadn't met him, I didn't hear loud music, flatulence or grunting coming through his walls...phew! I could however, hear him urinating like a cart horse regularly throughout the night. The first time I heard it I thought I had a leak and expected to see water flooding down my walls. Yep, I now had trumping, snoring and peeing to listen to, it was like sleeping next to a human percussion section of the worst orchestra in the world.

The only other downside to my house, was that unfortunately it only had a front garden so, when I got home from work in the summer, the only way I could get some much-needed sunshine was to sit at the front on my doorstep like some vagrant. I would get home, pour a glass of lovely cold *Pinot Grigio* and park my backside on the doorstep while Ferdinand wandered around the garden on his lead sniffing out the scents of the invaders who had dared to trespass on his lawn that day. I know. It isn't the best image, is it? Unfortunately, after long stressful days at work, the need for wine and sunshine out-weighed any concerns I may have had of looking like a right chav. All I needed to complete the image was a pink shellsuit, a tan the colour of Fuzzy Navel hangover pee, manicured nails that rival *Edward Scissorhands* and enough bling to look like I had raided Beaverbrooks.

I was sat there one day gulping the remains of my revitalising wine, when the new neighbour pulled up on his drive directly next to mine. He saw me and instantly got out and waltzed his burly frame over to introduce himself.

'Hi Hunny. I'm Rob. I've just moved in at the back of you.' Now as he said this perfectly innocent statement (apart from the 'Hunny' bit which was a tad forward on first meeting) he followed it up with a wink. Hmm…. I thought. Giving him the benefit of the doubt, perhaps he was one of these people who winks randomly at you at the end of every sentence.

'Hi, I'm Izzy and this is Ferdinand.' I had to introduce Ferdinand as, being a friendly dog, he was now trying to nuzzle his way into Rob's affection by trying to jump up and sniff his balls.

We continued to chat on; Rob worked as a security guard at a local building merchants, was 51, had two small children and was separated from his wife. How can somebody saying, 'I have two kids' come across as being an innuendo? But he managed it by following it with a wink. It's like he was saying, 'Yep my balls work fine, my semen swim like Michael Phelps and I have managed to produce two fine offspring. Do you fancy a shag?'

I gave him the benefit of the doubt again thinking that perhaps he had some sort of twitch that he was unaware of. Understandably, I didn't point his eye tick out, but if I had stood there much longer talking to him I was going to start mirroring his twitches right back. Needing to escape from this winkathon, I ended the conversation by saying that I'd better go and check on my tea, but it was nice to meet him… Polite as ever. He finished by saying 'Bye Hunny, I will no doubt see you again soon' Wink Wink…Yes! Double wink! Things were escalating!

I didn't see him then for about a week, it was a British summer after all so I was in and out of my house in the blink, or more appropriately wink, of an eye avoiding the downpours. It was only when the sun started to shine again that Winky Man came back into my life. On this particular night though, as the sun had gone down, I was sat in watching TV. As I don't have the vast array of channels that Sky or any of its rivals offer, my summer viewing was an option between the re-runs of *Midsomer Murders* or *Lewis,* which are great if you suffer from insomnia, or one of the plethora of reality programmes involving either has-been or wanna-be celebrities. Ooh! What a choice!

Anyway, while I was gripped trying to work out which of the elderly residents of *Midsomer* boring village-of –the-year was going to get bumped off next, I heard a knock at the door. Tearing myself reluctantly away from the intense drama unfolding as Inspector Barnaby removed the knitting needle from Miss Thorndike's neck, I was greeted by the sight of Mr Winky stood at my door in a shirt bright enough to give you a tension headache. No wonder he bloody twitched, my eyes started to spasm at the yellow apparition.

'Hi Hunny, I just thought I would pop round and

tell you that you have a wasp nest above your bedroom window.' Wink. Why he was looking up at my bedroom window I dreaded to think, but nonetheless it was a neighbourly thing to do.

'Oh thanks,' I said, 'I'll give the landlord a call and ask him to get somebody out to it.'

'Are you sure you don't want me to go up to your bedroom and have a look for you Hunny?' Wink. Tempting as the offer was to invite the winking Pacman upstairs, I politely declined saying it was okay thanks, I was sure the landlord would sort it. There was no bloody way he was getting up my stairs to checkout my eaves!

The next day I rang the landlord who arranged for a pest controller to come out to take a look at my problematic gable dwellers. Having inspected the swarm, the pest controller then rang me to say it wasn't wasps but bees; apparently these little stripy blighters are protected and therefore would need to remain inhabiting my roof space until they decide they'd had enough of Knutsford and packed up their little honey sacks and moved to a different location. To be honest they weren't bothering me, in fact the buzzing could come in handy!

When I got home from work that night Mr Winky Man's car was on the drive so I thought before I went in, I'd call round to update him about the buzzing squatters. As is the norm for this intelligent sophisticated office worker, I was wearing my office apparel consisting of a fitted black dress and patent high heels you could spear a trout with. On seeing me stood on his doorstep in all my finery he stared at me like a pubescent in a lap-dancing club and he then actually licked his lips… OMG, at this point I already knew this was a mistake and alarm bells started to ring in my head saying, *Ding! Think woman. Think!*

'Ooh! You look gorgeous today Hunny' Wink Wink, 'I like your dress…and those heels!' Wink Wink…Yes! Four winks in one sentence. This wasn't a good sign. However, me being me, I went straight into fluster mode ignoring the alarm bells that now sounded like a bunch of campanologists on Easter Sunday, and instead decided it would be far better to just not engage my brain at all before I spoke. So instead of just saying, 'Thank you' and taking the compliment, what did I say?

'Oh. I will be taking this off in a minute, you should see me then.' *Fuckety fuck! What in God's name did I say that for?* NOT the right thing to say to a man licking his lips at the thoughts of pleasuring me in my high heels. What I was really meaning, in my little incoherent world, was that I would be changing out of my work gear and into my scruffs once I got in the house, but it just came out like I was offering to take him to mine to perform a striptease.

Funny really, I've never seen somebody's eyes spasm in two different directions as he tried to wink and ogle my boobs at the same time; he looked like he was having some sort of wink-induced seizure. At this point he was now not only having thoughts about me standing in front of him in high heels, but as a Brucey bonus, he was imagining this scenario with me stark naked. I nearly had to wipe the drool from his open mouth.

Fearful that he was going to take me up on the offer to watch me peel my dress off, I then just proceeded to babble on with a face the colour of an overripe beetroot about how I'd just bobbed round to tell him it was a bees nest and unfortunately there wasn't anything that could be done. As I tottered off down the drive, with the sensation I was being watched more attentively than a pyromaniac in a fireworks factory, I had the feeling that by the time I had my key in the door, he would be in his own home giving his one-eyed chap a bit of a wink.

Our next brief encounter was a couple of weeks later as by some miracle, or more likely avoidance tactics that put me in the same league as a top MI5 special branch operative, I had repeatedly managed to dodge him.

It was the sort of rare summer evening where even the most antisocial hermits had to pop their heads outside to get some fresh air, so I was once again sat on the doorstep thinking that I really must buy a bench or put an old sofa out here so I could look like a proper chav!

The landlord had a gardener that supposedly came around to cut the grass at the front, but as he was about as regular as British Rail, the grass was now getting towards meadow status. It was only a matter of time before I'd be finding an old cardigan and an abandoned supermarket trolley hidden in the depths. Ferdinand liked it though as he mooched about through the long grass in search of any abandoned pieces of food he could snaffle.

As Mr Winky Man arrived home from work he sauntered over. Oh dear God!

'Hi my gorgeous little neighbour, how are you doing?' Wink. Gorgeous little neighbour…Really? Did he just say that?

'Fine thanks, and you?' I replied trying not to eye spasm in return.

'Yeah, I'm off work tomorrow so I'm going to cut my grass and I noticed yours is a bit long, do you want me to cut it for you?' Wink.

'Oh, that's nice of you but it's okay, the landlord does it, but thanks for the offer.'

At this point I think I should tell you that I also had a small shrub in my garden in front of my window. Now the reason why I'm explaining this isn't because I've suddenly turned into Knutsford's answer to Alan Tichmarsh, but it may help explain Winky Man's next comment.

'Okay Hunny, but do you want me to trim your bush for you?' Wink, Wink.

Eeeekkk! Had I suddenly been transported into a bad *Carry On* movie or did he not realise what he had said and was really just offering to cut the foliage on my shrubbery? I think we all know though he was being rude, don't we?

Having managed to not spurt wine all over him in

response, I stuttered, 'Erm thanks but it's okay. I can do it.' *Hell will freeze over and I will be ice-skating with the devil butt naked before you will get anywhere near my bush, mate.*

I again made some feeble excuse about 'potatoes not peeling themselves' in order to get away before he started to talk about his trimming skills.

However, the next night when I came home my bush HAD been thoroughly attacked and I now had something that resembled a bonsai tree and a rather bald one at that! Not wanting to seem unappreciative the next time I saw him I said,

'Thanks for cutting back the shrub'. See how I avoided the word bush there? I had listened to the campanologists ringing alarm bells this time and engaged my brain before speaking.

'Oh, it's no problem Hunny, I like a neat bush and you have a very tidy one now,' Wink Wink.

Good Grief. I was now expecting Frankie Howard to appear any minute from behind the wall going, 'Ooo-err Missus… Nice bush'. As I was a bit flustered, my brain decided now would be a good time to take a well-earned rest, leaving my mouth to articulate the response.

'Yeah it's much better thanks. You can see through my window now.' Oh, for goodness sake! What is wrong with me? Have I lost all capacity to think before I speak? Why did I say YOU can see through? What I meant was I could!

'Yeah Hunny,' Wink Wink 'I know,' Wink Wink.

Shit!!! I had done it again…I'd achieved a quadruple wink with a triple summersault eye spasm. I now had to keep my blinds partially shut for fear that he was stood over the road with a pair of high powered binoculars pinned to his twitching peepers in the hope of glimpsing me stripping off my work dress to reveal my neatly trimmed bush.

11

G'day Sheila ... or is it Bruce?

One of the hardest things when I became footloose and fancy-free again, was deciding what the hell I was going to do with all the leave that I had stacking up quicker than letters in a postal strike. I now had more days off to use than the president of the Jimmy Savile fan club. I'm not quite at the age where a coach trip to the Outer Hebrides, consisting of a quick stop off at the Edinburgh woollen mill factory to pick up a nice tweed pleated skirt, is that appealing.

Mind you, on the other hand, thoughts of going on a singles holiday was equally daunting given the calibre of the goons I'd met so far. A full week of being offered to have my brains surgically removed by some inebriated Romeo's penis, made me think that perhaps just a quiet week in the Lake District with a dog, a vibrator, a shed load of chocolate and a few boxes of wine was the closest thing to a holiday I was going to get.

Don't you just love those boxes of wine? I'm not a wine snob, so the fact that you are blissfully unaware of how much you have actually drunk is great. Unlike the bottle where you can see the liquid evaporating at an alarming rate, the hidden contents of the box will lull you into a false sense of sobriety; it easily kids you into thinking that you have only had a couple of squeezes, until your slurred attempt at speaking tells you otherwise. As an added bonus, when you get to the point where you think it's finished, you can perform a box autopsy and surgically remove the innards which will enable you to squeeeeeeeze another glass out by playing it like a wine bagpipe. Small pleasures eh?

My holiday salvation came as I took the decision to bravely ask my friend Em if I could go and visit her in Australia for a couple of weeks in January. I'd been out there once previously but going on my own, well that was a totally different prospect. What was I thinking? I can't even manage to get to the shops without a mishap, so was going to the other side of the world on my own really a sensible idea? Nevertheless, Em was really excited at the thought, and it was just what I needed, so I booked the flights, applied for the visa and started to panic about how I would manage to find my way from Manchester to Sydney with a stopover in Abu Dhabi without creating an international incident.

I'd always been quite an organised person; whenever the family went away I used to take control of the packing to ensure we all had colour co-ordinated clothes in each of the cases. This was to minimise the prospect of one of us losing all our clothes if the cases ended up in Tanzania instead of Tenerife, thus leaving whoever with only the sweaty clothes they were travelling in. If you are ever unfortunate enough to get your case mislaid by the airport baggage lottery, then you can be assured that the insurance budget will only allow you to buy the bare minimum: a pair of flip-flops that would rival the cheese-grater sandals in the comfort stakes, elasticated shorts that are only popular with the over 70s or the obese, and a couple of vest tops that say 'I love the Canaries' on the back that will immediately stretch to ridiculous proportions so will only fit a lopsided hunchback when washed.

My packing for Australia demonstrated just how much my life had changed. This time I threw in more or less everything from my wardrobe on the morning of departure, praying that my now hefty case did not exceed the extensive weight limit, and trusting that the two bikinis I had scoured the winter shops for, were actually in there somewhere.

Have you ever tried to buy a bikini or any other beach gear in January? As it's winter sale time, they put out all the unsold garments that were fashionable two years ago, and still didn't sell. Either that or everything on the rails is made of wool, fur, is fleecy-lined or has so much bling on it that even the most ostentatious rapper would have a problem carrying it off. This made the task of locating decent, or in fact any, summer gear harder than finding the abominable snowman in an avalanche...bloody impossible. My options were therefore limited to the poor selection available for the out of season and ill-prepared traveller. Even my trip to Primark, where you can usually buy a whole new wardrobe full of clothes at any time of year for little more than a side dish at Yo Sushi was unsuccessful.

When I did eventually find some swimsuits tucked away in the corner, where only the most intrepid shopper ventures, I made my way to the changing rooms. Oh God. I then had to try the sodding thing on when for weeks I'd done zilch but eat highly calorific food and drink copious amounts of alcohol. All this whilst doing nothing more exerting than opening a particularly tricky box of chocolates and flicking the remote to watch re-runs of poor Christmas specials.

Buying swimwear is never a great experience when you look in those brightly lit mirrors to see yourself from every conceivable angle, but buying one with a flabby Christmas pudding belly and a sun deprived arse that resembles the surface of the moon on a bright night, filled me with such self-doubt that I had the urge to cancel the holiday and book myself into rehab. In the end, I did manage to find one that covered my backside just enough to hide the particularly dimply bits; I therefore bought it in two colours.

With my throw-it-all-in packing completed, and my passport safely stowed in my bag alongside the Nytol for the plane, I tried to calm my nerves for the journey ahead as I made my way to the airport. How hard can this be? They won't let me on the wrong plane and I can read (although maybe not Arabic) so all I need to do is concentrate and ask if I'm stuck… I AM an intelligent woman… Oh shit. I was soooooo scared!

I arrived at the airport dragging my wardrobe on wheels with me and made my way to the check-in desk. Good start, it was easy to find and there was no queue. I handed my passport and e-ticket to the pleasant looking highly coutured lad on the desk and awaited the routine questions. I only started to get a teeny-weeny bit concerned when these questions were not forthcoming and the highly polished face of the check-in attendant took on a puzzled look similar to Joey Essex at …well pretty much at everything in life really.

'I'm sorry Mrs Parkes,' he said, 'but there seems to be a bit of a discrepancy with your ticket'. Oh bum here we go!

'Oh. Erm why?'

'Well your ticket is in the name of Mr Isobel Parkes, so I was just checking that it was your ticket.' Bum and Bollocks. I haven't even got on the flight and already my cock-ups are coming back to haunt me.

'Let me just check for you, I'm sure it's nothing to worry about.' Tell that to your face mate, as his expression took on a 'What the hell do I do' look.

He must have seen my panic as he swiftly added, 'I'm sure it will be fine but I just need to confirm that it's just an oversight and you will be okay travelling.'

This lad really needed to take acting lessons if he was going to pull off a performance that was no more convincing than when Bill Clinton said, 'Monica who?' I managed to get out a strangled, 'Thanks' that sounded more like a cross between a cry and a squawk as he scuttled off, undoubtedly looking for somebody who had come across this situation before. This left me to anxiously contemplate the possible alternatives of having to either a) buy a new ticket (expensive) b) pay to get it changed (less expensive) or, God forbid c) not get on the flight (Not an option at all!).

I stood there deliberating what I could pawn to pay for a new flight. The only option I was coming up with was to put it on the credit card and then look into selling something when I got home. Hmm…as I had nothing that would fetch more than a fiver on eBay, it came down to either selling a kidney or my body. As the second option may take me some considerable time and effort, my own body weight in condoms and a ton of vodka to get through it, it all came down to flogging a kidney. Fortunately, before I had time to worry about functioning through life with one less organ, the young lad returned this time accompanied by a bloke who looked like a Village People reject in his airport uniform and neatly trimmed moustache. Oh Bugger! This was not a good sign, and to make things worse, I now had YMCA playing in my head.

'Hello Mrs Parkes. I'm sorry to have kept you waiting. It seems that there has been a slight error on the ticket, however, as the name's correct and it's just the title that's wrong, we've checked with the airlines and confirmed that you will be fine travelling on the ticket.'

Oh my God, I wanted to kiss Mr Village People there and then I was so relieved. I'm not sure he would have appreciated it though and, as the ferret looking moustache resting on his top lip contained what looked like a bit of regurgitated blueberry muffin, I'm not sure I fancied it either really. So, instead of launching myself at him, I just opted for the more restrained and traditional way of conveying my appreciation to a total stranger.

Having now completed the check in as Mr Parkes, my bulging case was labelled with a big orange HEAVY sticker and loaded onto the conveyor belt with the aid of a winch and a muscular attendant. It was a good job I'd left that pair of orange shoes at home or I was sure I'd have been over the already generous allowance. It's always a nervous moment when they weigh your baggage, although maybe not as tense as when you weigh yourself after the holiday.

Thank God, I wasn't travelling with one of the budget airlines though. I've only ever done that once and what an experience that was. I stood in a queue the length of the Great Wall of China, watching people frantically pack and unpack their suitcases due to being half a gram over the weight allowance, which was going to cost them more than the flight itself. It was like a Primark sale in the terminal with underwear and cheap vest tops strewn across the floor while people swapped items or spent five minutes deciding if they could do without the flip-flops or the push up bra for the week. If you're interested the push up bra went in, the girl in question grabbed both her ample bosoms and, thrusting them up like they were a couple of water balloons, stated, 'Well these two babies are going to get me more drinks than a pair of flip-flops will.' You can't argue with the logic there, can you?

With my hefty case on its journey through the mysterious world of luggage loading, I made my way to security, safe in the knowledge that I had followed all the stringent guidelines required to board a plane these days; all my toiletries were of the legal-size requirement and were correctly stored in a see-through zip lock bag obtained in advance. See, I can be organised. Surprisingly there wasn't much of a queue, I guess Friday night wasn't the busiest time for travelling as all the business flyers had made their way home so, apart from the odd long-haul flight, there were not many departures.

As I sat in the bar feeling slightly apprehensive to say the least, I was asking myself the same question that I'm sure we all ponder when boarding a plane: 'I wonder who I'll be sat next to?' This is bad enough when it's a short flight and you're travelling with somebody, but add into the equation that you're a lone traveller and, whoever the gods of chance sit you next to will be your companion for at least the next eight hours, the question becomes all the more important. The trick is to try and not look too conspicuous as you covertly scan the surrounding areas in an effort to spot your potential fellow passengers.

As I surreptitiously surveyed the scene, I ticked off the people in my head who I thought looked like they were about to embark on the same epic journey. First to catch my eye was an overweight sweaty bloke.

Although the seating area is slightly bigger for long haul flights, it would still be a squeeze to get his considerable frame in one seat. The flab that was now making an attempt to escape over the top of his trousers, would no doubt end up spilling onto my side enveloping me in a sea of fat. Add to that the fact that he was perspiring like a weight-watcher in a cake shop, and the thoughts of spending a number of hours pinned in half of my seat while trying to avoid the sweaty blubber did not fill me with joy.

Next in my line of sight was a young couple with a baby. Now, although the parents looked happy and calm, coo-cooing at their lovely little baby who watched on with an amiable toothless smile, this would not last. I've spent a couple of hours on a plane with a baby myself and, although you try your hardest to keep them awake so they sleep on the flight, this rarely happens; the minute those engines start to whir into life, so does the baby. They become possessed by the Airplane Baby Devil turning them into a screaming crying mass of mucus and tears. They will then spend the entire flight awake but getting so tired and irritable that even Mr Bunnikins and a mouth full of dummies will not sooth the poor little thing…until ten minutes before landing when they will fall into a peaceful sleep. The parents will come off wondering what the hell just happened and looking rougher than if they'd just spent the night on a bender in the company of Charlie Sheen.

As I looked at the calm and happy family scene in front of me now though, I wasn't too worried about being seated next to them. Why? Well I have a little tip for you when choosing your seat on a long-haul flight; if you want to avoid babies steer clear of booking the bulk head seats. Now, I know this seems odd, as surely this will give you more room to stretch your aching limbs during the flight. But do this at your peril, as this is where any savvy parent will book their seats so that they can have the in-flight cots assembled at the front. On a busy flight, there could be more babies around you than at the local maternity ward so, yes, your legs will think they have won the leg lottery, but your ears and nerves will be shredded as every piercing cry bounces off your brain leaving you feeling like you have just been subjected to eight hours of the latest sleep deprivation technique.

As I continued my furtive reconnaissance I spotted a lone drunk pale-looking woman.. Oh shit, that's a mirror.

The only other potentially problematic companions that I'd seen were a mother and toddler. This was an even worse scenario than the baby as you can't predict where these little blighters are going to sit… if they sit at all!

Now, you may be thinking at this point that I

don't like children, but this isn't the case. I just don't want to be in a confined space with them while they get so bored that kicking your seat, running up and down the aisle or throwing toys over at you, becomes entertainment for them.

As I sat there nursing my second glass of wine, I tried to suss out if the Mum looked like she could control the little girl enough to make sure she didn't spend the flight annoying the crap out of fellow passengers. By the looks of things, I was likely to need copious amounts of drink if she was near me, as the pink diva stamped her feet and then threw herself on the floor because she didn't want to drag her case shaped like a mutant pink cat any further. Great!

When the departures board eventually changed to Go to Gate for my flight, I downed the dregs of my wine before paying a final visit to a toilet that didn't sound like it was about to suck you through the U-bend into oblivion when you flushed it. As I sat at the gate waiting to board, I noticed that the pleasant family with the currently unpossessed baby, the Mum with the tantruming toddler and the fat sweaty bloke were all amongst the people congregating around the restricted seating area waiting to be called to board the plane.

Before the ground staff had finished the word 'Could…' people were immediately up and out of their seats like they were under starters orders for the 100 meters. They then started to form a large queue pushing to try to get in first like the plane was going to leave without them if they were not stood in line within a minute of the announcement. You got others like me, who sat there in amusement watching as somebody just sauntered up and joined the party at the front to the sound of tutting from the people behind. Personally, I've always wondered why people feel the need to queue when you already have your seat allocated. Obviously, this excludes some of the budget airlines where you take your life in your own hands in a battle of epic proportions between pushchairs and wheelie suitcases with scenes only rivalled by a Black Friday Sale at TK Maxx.

As this was not a first-come first-served arrangement though, getting on the plane within a nano-second of the gates opening would not make a monkey's chuff to how early we left, or who you were destined to spend the next eight hours practically conjoined to, so why bother? So, it was with this ethos that I sat there patiently watching the queue dwindle until I felt it was time to face my fate and approach the desk to hand over my ticket as 'Mr Parkes'. The look on the pleasantly smiling young girl at the departure gate quickly changed to a state of confusion as she looked at the name on the ticket. Still, after a brief explanation as to why it was that I was travelling as a man, she let me through, much to my relief.

Now the big question would be answered. Please not the toddler, please not the toddler. Yay! It was a normal looking bloke with no kids, no excess blubber and a friendly face, the gods of chance had been good to me…or maybe not. As I began to remove the blanket and complimentary flying pack containing the essentials for the flight, all I could hear from somewhere behind me was, 'No honey, come from under the seat. You need to sit down' followed by, 'Oh sweetie, don't put those up your nose they are for your ears'. I had a feeling I would be needing mine….

The bloke next to me seemed quite nice and, now I'd had the chance to get a better look, was actually quite good-looking. Wahoo! As we settled into our seats we engaged in the sort of mundane small talk that's required when you're sat next to somebody on a plane, 'Where are you going to?' 'How long for?' 'Have you flown with this airline before?' You can then move on to idle chit-chat about 'What do you do?' 'Where do you live?' 'Isn't the weather cold?' …. 'I wish that kid would shut the hell up!'

Yes, we were having a very pleasant chat while the plane ascended to God knows how many thousand feet to the sounds of, 'Pumpkin, don't hit that nice man on the head' and, 'Darling, stop kicking the seat or the pretty lady in the uniform will come and tell you off'. I wished the pretty lady in the uniform would come and put the little monster in the baggage hold and give us all a nice flight. The fella next to me, whom I now knew was called Peter, rolled his eyes at yet another pathetic attempt by the mother to stop the unruly toddler from undoing her seatbelt for the ninetieth time and standing on the seat. 'Little Lucy' was now in serious danger of being walloped by the man directly in front of her who was obviously struggling to control himself at being slapped on his bald head while the toddler said, 'Bang, bang, bang'. To all our relief the fasten seat belt sign pinged off and Lucy's Mum quickly whisked her little princess away to go and see the pretty lady at the front. Further relief was obtained by the arrival of the drinks trolley when the slapped bald-headed bloke ordered two bottles of white wine with a whisky chaser. Christ, this was going to be a long flight.

I now settled down to watch a garbage action movie with some past it stars trying to re-capture their youth in a half action packed thriller that I can't even recall the name of. I love a good action movie but there comes a point in a man's life when he stops looking like an action hero and looks more like he should be down the allotment in a string vest fighting with a stubborn asparagus than pretending that he can jump from a fourth-floor window to battle with a trained assassin half his age. Still, it passed a couple of hours and meant I didn't have to listen to further sickly admonishments of 'Lucifer the toddler devil'.

The arrival of the neatly packaged airline food, and yet more wine, meant that Peter and I chatted a bit more about our lives and what we were going to be doing on our trip. It turned out he had a sister in Abu Dhabi and was going to stay with her for a couple of weeks as he hadn't had a break since his divorce last year.

Yep, single, nice and not bad looking, things were looking up. The flight continued in a cycle of film, chat, drink, stretch my legs, wee, food, choke on circulated fumes from someone's backside, all whilst listening to Lucifer being told to, 'Sit down baby'. The bald bloke was so inebriated by the end of the flight that he could have been slapped on the head by a team of Bavarian folk dancers and he wouldn't have cared.

As we made our descent into Abu Dhabi, Peter asked if he could have my number so he could give me a ring and perhaps meet up when we both got back. As he'd been pleasant company, didn't have breath that could strip paint at 40 paces nor had he said anything that made me think he was a complete moron, it didn't take me long to decide, 'Yes'. What did I have to lose?

You know that quote from Forrest Gump: 'Mama always said life was like a box of chocolates. You never know what you're gonna get'? Well after saying my goodbyes to Peter, who I would perhaps compare to a smooth and delicious milk chocolate truffle, I then met Doris who was definitely more like a coffee cream with a bit of the chocolate missing.

Abu Dhabi is not the easiest of airports to negotiate when you need to connect to your next flight. Erring on the side of caution, I decided to join the queue at the flight information desk to make sure I didn't end up wandering around the airport in a vain attempt to work out in Arabic where people on transfer flights were supposed to go; I wasn't taking any chances I had to get that flight.

As I stood in the queue waiting patiently, I sensed somebody had joined behind me, so turning around to check I wasn't about to be assaulted by Lucifer, I was greeted by a friendly 'G'Day... It's a bit of a long queue isn't it darlin?' Bloody hell! A stunted Dame Edna had joined the queue behind me.

Now, I'm not exactly tall myself, but the lady who stood somewhere just below my eye line behind me had seriously missed out in the feet and inches department. I wouldn't call her a dwarf but if Charlie needed some additional umpa lumpas for his chocolate factory she was a definite candidate.

'Oh yes, it is, but it seems to be moving quickly so hopefully we shouldn't be here too long,' I say helpfully and hopefully.

'Where you off to darlin?'

Tempting as it was to reply in my best Dame Edna voice, *'Well my little possum I'm going to Sydney in search of a didgeridoo'* I just said,

'I'm travelling to Sydney. Where are you off to?' I like to ask the bleeding obvious given the woman had the strongest Antipodean accent I'd heard since *Neighbours.*

'Oh, that's great darlin', I'm off to Sydney too. We can find where we're going together, as I really haven't a clue and tend to get more lost than a dingo with his nose cut off.'

'Yeah that'll be good' I said, smiling convincingly whilst thinking Bugger...I've done it again, I've managed to attract the only stray in the airport with a worse sense of direction than me.

She then proceeded to tell me all about the trip she'd been on to Ireland where she'd somehow managed, to meet a bloke who she referred to as her boyfriend. Do you have boyfriends when you're in your 50s? Anyway, as we queued and then trundled around the airport in search of a seat to park our backsides, I was subjected to the life and loves of Doolally Doris who, it turned out, was dating an ex-IRA terrorist who had served a number of years in jail during The Troubles in Ireland in the 1980s. She couldn't go into details of his crime (thank God) as she said it was all very Top Secret, but he had been high up in the IRA and, needless to say, had not deserved his incarceration because it had all been a set up.. Hmm to quote Mandy Rice-Davies, 'Well, he would say that, wouldn't he?'

This association with the IRA, and his criminal record meant, however, that he would be unable to come and visit her since he was banned from travelling to most countries. I'm not sure if the tale he had spun her was true, or if he just wanted to somehow embellish his past and avoid making the journey to see her, but I can tell you one thing; this lady was hooked. She was determined; she was going back to see the new love of her life, once he had sent her his new address after he'd moved in a couple of months. Ahh bless, I had a feeling that maybe it didn't all work out quite as she'd imagined.

At the time though, I was not feeling quite so

sympathetic. I swear that my ears had started to bleed from the high-pitched inane chatter that they were being subjected to. I had only managed the odd, 'Hmmm' and, 'Oh dear' and, 'I know' as the woman went on and on. Once we had exhausted tales of her trip she then proceeded to tell me all about her life in Tasmania, the neighbour with one leg who was feeding her seven cats (named after the seven dwarfs – hmmm appropriate), the number of ornaments she had and the hand-made display cabinets they were kept in. She also then went on to recount how she had been affected by the awful fires that swept through the local area, and finally her hysterectomy the previous year that meant she was now on HRT causing her to gain over a stone in the last few months. Good lord! Is there nothing she hadn't told me? Her poor neighbour probably chewed her own leg off in an attempt to dull the pain of being subjected to more than a few hours of relentless drivel.

Finally, it was time to set off to the gate, which turned out to be a three-day camel ride away…and this woman was seriously unfit. Not only was she carrying the extra stone but she was also now having trouble breathing whilst maintaining a pace that a snail on dope could have beaten. Great. I was now escorting an asthmatic dwarf with verbal diarrhoea whilst lugging both her leopard skin holdall and mine to the departure gate, all the while still listening to yet more monotonous tales about how her local supermarket gives her a really good deal on cat litter. My ears were now in meltdown. The only saving grace was that I knew for certain that she wasn't sat next to me on the plane as she had already asked me my seat number. Thank fuck!!

Now, do you remember me saying that I could never understand people who queued to get on a plane when you have your seat allocated? I now take that back, as I shot out of my seat, quicker than a greyhound out of a trap, at the first sign of boarding. Unbelievably, she still managed to follow me into the queue, despite her slowness on the walk it now seemed she had the sprinting ability of a sprightly gazelle. Had I just been conned into carrying her bags I wondered? She now proceeded to tell me how she never slept on flights; well colour me purple and call me Barney, no bloody surprise there, eh? Still at least once I was in the sanctuary of the plane my ears could spend the next 14 hours in recovery, unlike the poor bastard she'd be sat next to who would no doubt need noise cancelling headphones to stand any chance of sleep.

I hadn't even thought about who my flight companion would be, THAT is how bad she was; anybody would be better surely. Fortunately, the gods of chance were kind, having spent the last three hours pissing themselves laughing at my misfortune, they decided that enough was enough and kindly gave me a Dutch bloke who hardly spoke… Ahhh peace!

The second leg of the flight again consisted of a rotation of food, sleep, wine, wee, movie until we landed safely on terra firma in Sydney. As I wearily disembarked though, I thought I was back in Manchester. It was grey, dull and raining, although ever so slightly warmer. Where was the Australian sunshine I had been promised? It hadn't rained since Christmas day and now it was coming down in buckets. Never mind, I'd made it in one piece, my ears were no longer in shell shock and all I had to do was get through customs to meet Em who was waiting for me.

Having trundled with my cumbersome case and hand baggage out into the busy airport, I frantically scanned the sea of faces for my best friend, and there she was, waving and jumping about like some epileptic lunatic in front of me………….

God, it was sooooooo good to see her that all thoughts of the past 24 hours spent getting there evaporated in an instant. This was going to be so much fun.

12

It's Big, it's Hairy and it's Bloody Scary!

It was like the parting of the Red Sea as we ploughed our way through the crowds of eagerly waiting friends and relatives with my large orange stickered suitcase leading the way. Fortunately, it wasn't far to the car and more importantly Em's partner Harry was there to negotiate lifting the ten-ton case into the vehicle.

I'm sure he wondered if I'd actually emigrated I had that much stuff, but his worried look soon turned to pleasure when I presented him with a large bottle of Vanilla Absolut. I had a feeling that he'd probably be needing something to numb the experience as the plan was for me to stay with them for a week, and then it was off for a girly holiday on Hamilton Island, on the Great Barrier Reef, with a final night in Sydney to finish… Perfect.

It was a two-and-a-half-hour drive to Em's and in that time, it never stopped raining, and we never stopped talking. I reckon we'd have given Doolally Doris a run for her money in the Talking Shite Stakes.

Having unpacked my year's worth of clothes,

cramming them unceremoniously into the two drawers and half a wardrobe that Em had generously spared for me, we then just sat on the covered decking watching the rain, drinking beer and catching up. It felt so good to see her again, I don't think we came up for air.

You know when you're so tired that your eyeballs feel like they've been sandblasted and then dipped in vinegar? Well by about nine o'clock that was exactly how I felt, as the combination of tiredness and alcohol took over my jet-lagged little brain telling me to bugger off to bed before it went into shut-down mode.

It's not a big city where Em lives and, although it's not out in the sticks, the prospect of snakes, poisonous spiders and ones the size of dinner plates are a reality. For this wimpy Pom this was always something that put me off visiting. Although our British spiders are ugly buggers, the worse thing they can do is stare at you in a threatening way before you squash them. Their Antipodean cousins however, are vicious blighters that lurk menacingly under the toilet seat patiently waiting until your pasty white butt appears …then BAM! The little bastard gets ya. It's for this reason that, despite my tiredness, I did a sweep of the bedroom like a bomb disposal expert, looking in every nook and cranny for any critters that may be lurking. I then practically stripped the bed before getting in, safe in the knowledge that there were no dangerous creatures ready to kill me in my sleep.

The next morning, having dragged myself out of

bed, still a little bit groggy from both jet lag and beer head, I was pleased to see that the rain had gone and been replaced by a gloriously clear blue sky. Em had to work for the first few days of my visit which meant that I could adjust to the new time zone and chill by the pool reading my book and sleeping in the shade. Lovely, and just what I needed. Evenings were spent chatting and having a couple of wines before retiring to bed at a decent hour for a good night's kip…well that was until the third morning came around.

I woke up at about three o'clock needing a pee, I put this off for a while not wanting to wake anybody, but in the end, I gave up realising I wouldn't get back to sleep unless I went. Groggily I put the lamp on next to the bed so I could see where I was going…OH HOLY MOTHER OF GOD!! There, perched on the door frame, was the biggest spider I had seen in my entire life! It was that big you could have put a lead on it and taken it for a walk in the park and it would have given any medium-sized dog a run for its money.

I didn't know what the hell I was going to do, as it was guarding the doorway like some arachnid bouncer on steroids. By this time, I was fully awake and obviously, the need had become more pressing as the fear of being trapped in the bedroom by this monster took over my bladder. If I opened the door to get out it would surely start to scuttle in one direction or another and it would no doubt end up heading right at me in an attempt to eat my face off…a tad dramatic I know, but when you're in a state of sheer panic these things pop into your mind. I mulled over this dilemma for some time trying to think of different scenarios that meant I could relieve myself without having to face my foe.

I could climb out of the window and go in a bush. No, there could be equally bad or maybe even worse things out there at this time in the morning and, even though the sight of my terrifying white backside descending on them would probably scare off most things, I wasn't going to take the chance.

An alternative could be to pee into something. For women though, this is a challenge at the best of times. Without the fine tuning required to direct the flow into any container, I could easily end up wetting the carpet, especially as the only thing I could see was a half empty glass that I would fill quicker than a bucket at the bottom of Niagara Falls. Also, the big bugger would still be in the room so this wasn't an option.

I could always shout for help. It was far too early though, and besides, the minute they opened the door the hairy fiend would no doubt head in my direction again and start eating my face off… God, I really needed a pee!!!

The urge to relieve myself inevitably won over fear though; I had now stared at the furry legged beast for that long I'd actually given him a name – he was now called Boris. I felt that he deserved to have a name and in my deliriously panicked state, I thought that if I gave him the same name as the equally dishevelled Mr

Johnson, it would make him seem less intimidating.

Did it work? Of course, it bloody didn't… he was still a big fat hairy-legged ugly spider. In the end, I finally came up with a plan from the Baldrick book of cunning plans. My brainwave was to take a large towel, which was within reaching distance, and throw it over Boris thus trapping him underneath. I would then be able to move the towel and get out. Good plan eh? Hmmm. I know. Shit plan, but it was the best I could come up with as the need to urinate became increasingly urgent.

Grabbing the towel with shaking hands I took aim, after all how could I miss, he was taking up half the doorway. I watched with horror as the towel launched through the air landing squarely…next to him. It did however manage to catch him a glancing blow that sent him thundering off to the side under a cupboard. OH, SWEET JESUS, he was now in hiding ready to pounce when I passed, but at least the doorway was clear so I took the opportunity to dart out to the bathroom… Ahhhhhh momentary relief.

My problem now, however, was that Boris was still holed up in my bedroom. This called for a new strategy, which was basically to keep a watchful eye on the cupboard where he'd taken refuge. When Harry eventually got up he would then be able to capture the creature with a lasso and trawlerman's net. I cautiously went back into the bedroom with the stealth of a ninja walking into a room of eggshells just in case my enemy had emerged from his hiding place and was ready to seek his revenge. I then began my vigil during which time Boris did not appear once! I'm sure I could sense him staring back at me intensely eyeing his prey…or was that just my imagination again?

'HARRY!!! I need you in here now. There's a big ugly spider the size of a small mongrel under the cupboard'.

These were the first words out of my mouth the millisecond I heard movement in the house. I bet Harry's never been summoned into a woman's bedroom with that line before. To his credit, he dashed in expecting to see some big bugger with the cupboard attached to its back. However, the elusive git was evidently in no hurry to be evicted and had obviously fooled me at some point by making his escape to a different location with skills David Blane would be proud of.

So, we began the search…Okay, maybe not we, Harry, moved the cupboard, looked underneath, took the drawers out and all the contents, looked under the dressing table, moved the bed, looked in the wardrobe… well, you get the picture… he searched every nook and cranny of that bedroom and still the bugger was nowhere to be found. How can you not find a spider THAT big? Boris the illusionist had performed a disappearing act of epic proportions. Harry evidently thought that I was exaggerating the size of the beast and made the assumption that I was either still drunk, or Boris had made his escape from the room while I was in the bathroom. I, however, was not as convinced so spent a very restless time in bed the following night, keeping the light on; surely that would keep him at bay?

I began to relax marginally the following day, after all there had been no sign of it since I'd side-swiped him with a fluffy towel, so the likelihood was that he had scarpered while I was relieving myself in the bathroom. Following another hard day's drinking, enjoying the sunshine and relaxing by the pool I retired to bed in an almost catatonic state.

HOLY COCKING HELL! As I switched the light on there he was, loitering menacingly just above my bed. He just stared at me with a look that said, 'Come on then bitch if you think you're hard enough!' whist flexing the muscles in his huge hairy legs.

'HAAAAAARRRRRYYYYYYY. He's back!!!!!' I shouted at the top of my voice. I wasn't going to lose the bugger this time…no way…. it was me or him.

Harry raced in and stopped short at the sight of the huntsman spider currently taking up half the wall above my bed like some bizarre modern art sculpture. 'Jesus, he's a big bastard isn't he?' Nowt like stating the obvious, but it did at least give me some satisfaction to know that I had not been exaggerating and he was in fact not 'incy bloody wincy' as Harry had been calling him.

'He's the biggest I've seen since we moved to this house, that's for sure. I don't know if he'll fit in my spider capturing device.'

Now, I don't want you thinking that this was some great piece of Antipodean engineering that Australians have designed for trapping spiders the size of a Yorkshire terrier. No, this was a Tupperware container that had been adapted by Harry so that he could trap any arachnids and then release them away from the house. Personally, I would have just sprayed the git with spider killing spray.

'Take a picture before I get rid of him.' Harry said, as he too was now obviously impressed at the size of the bugger.

'Go and put your hand next to him to get some perspective of how big he is.' What? Did he think I had consumed so much alcohol I had now become Steve Irwin's replacement?

'Oh yeah right, because I really am that stupid. Why don't I just stand next to him and put my arm around him!'

I did take a picture of him, and to be fair, although he looked like he could give Quasimodo a run for his money in the ugly stakes, it didn't do his monstrous size justice. Still, at the cost of having heart failure and possibly my face eaten off from standing within one foot of the mean bastard, I was happy with this.

After a nervous approach, Harry just about managed to get Boris into his Tupperware contraption, although a couple of his legs did take a bit of a bashing so he could well have been scurrying with a slight limp after that. I gave Harry and his hairy captive an extremely wide berth as he passed; I made bloody sure he went to the bottom of the garden to release him though, as I didn't want him limping his way back up to break the door down with his six good legs so he could seek his revenge in the middle of the night.

Despite my earlier fatigue, sleep eluded me for some time that night as I lay there sweating, cocooned under the duvet with my eyes peeled watching for him to miraculously navigate a return. Of course, he didn't. Not that night, or any of the others that followed, but be assured, my encounter with Boris has certainly cured me of any fear I had of his puny British cousins.

13

Ssshunssshine in Paradise

After spending a mainly relaxing week, I said my goodbyes to Harry, as Em and I set off on our adventure to the Great Barrier Reef. I'm sure I could see the relief on his face as we drove off knowing that he would now be able to get his house back in some sort of order without two women disrupting his world and using all the toilet paper. Non-stop cricket and football interrupted only by food and beer beckoned for the next few days.

After a bumpy two-hour flight from Sydney, we arrived at Hamilton Island's airport. Well, when I say airport, I think the term that would be more appropriate is air hut. Good grief, I've seen bigger sheds on display at B&Q than the building that constituted the arrivals terminal.

There was no such thing as a baggage carousel here, just a sweaty bloke in a boiler suit with a trolley for you to find your precariously balanced case. It was like case Kerplunk trying to retrieve yours without dislodging the pile above it onto your head; health and safety was obviously not a concept they were familiar with.

The other thing that hit me as we got off the plane was the heat; as soon as I poked my head out of the door my eyelids began to sweat more than a sumo's scrotum. I even started to wonder if teeth could sweat I was so engulfed by the overwhelming humidity that slapped me in the face like a damp flannel. It wasn't particularly sunny; in fact, the skies looked perilously dark meaning that a downpour was due any time soon.

Having successfully retrieved our cases we made our way through the air hut to find our holiday rep stood with a sign displaying Em's name. It looked as though this had been hastily scrawled on two fag packets fastened together, it's just a good job Hubert Blaine Wolfeschlegelsteinhausenbergerdorff wasn't landing that day or she may have needed to smoke a few more packs. The other unusual thing about this little idyllic island was that it has no cars whatsoever. If you don't want to walk everywhere, the only way to get about was driving the golf buggies that are provided when you booked the accommodation. We'd just about managed to pile our cases on the back of ours when the heavens opened…and boy did they open. I'd never seen rain like it as it tumbled from the skies in a biblical downpour that would have had Noah shouting, 'Get those animals in pairs and on the boat sharpish'.

As Em had been to the island before, she decided it was best if she drove the buggy to our apartment. This was just fine with me as it was like trying to steer an oversized roller skate through a cascading torrent of water while somebody dowsed you with a hosepipe and threw buckets of water in your face at the same time. *It's a Knockout* sprung to mind as we negotiated our way on the sodden roads. To say we looked bedraggled when we arrived at the apartment was an understatement, even my underwear was feeling a bit damp but, as I stood there on the balcony looking out across the ocean, all thoughts of my soggy undercarriage disappeared. WOW! It was stunning even in the rain.

Em had booked the accommodation as my birthday present and it was amazing, not only for the spectacular view across the ocean, but the apartment itself was gorgeous and, most importantly of all, it had air-conditioning.

We each had our own bedroom and bathroom, which is always a plus as Em does have a tendency to snore like a truffle-hunting porker when she's hot and been drinking. I remember once when we shared a room on a trip to Barcelona, God almighty the ear-plugs, pillow and duvet over my head were still not enough to drown out the noise reverberating out of her nasal passages, and THEN, she had the cheek in the morning to say she hadn't slept well. You can imagine my response as I lay there looking bog-eyed and ever so slightly irritated, the words, 'Sodding', 'fooled', 'you could have' and 'me' were all used to convey my feelings quite adequately. Anyway, there was to be no repeat of this here as her bedroom wasn't within snoring distance; it was located at the other side of the apartment.

By the time we'd unpacked and re-showered, the torrential downpour had stopped but, as we walked out from the cool air-conditioned apartment onto the balcony, we were greeted by a wave of humidity that I can only imagine would be like walking into a pre-heated oven set on gas mark 7. There was a slight breeze, but unfortunately this too was warm, so rather than have a nice cooling effect, all this actually did was blow dry my already straw like hair into a style that you would only ever see in the weekly magazine *Farmers Choice*... And as for Em, no amount of Frizz Ease and conditioner was going to stop her head looking like an explosion in a cheap wig factory.

After drinking a glass of cool wine to replace the lost liquid we'd expunged during the short time we'd sat on the balcony, we made our way in the golf buggy down the road to the small cluster of bars and restaurants. Although drinking and driving is not something either of us would ever condone or do in a car, driving a golf buggy where you can be out-raced by a mobility scooter with a puncture whilst carrying an elephant, was okay. Let's face it, the most dangerous thing that can happen is that you run over somebody's toe and only if they had the reactions of a stunned tortoise to be unable to get out of the way.

As usual, we dithered - in our indecisive manner - about which bar to go in, but once we'd chosen and purchased our *Pinot*, we found a couple of high barstools overlooking the marina and settled ourselves in to admire the view, talk nonsense and watch the world go by. Bliss.

As we sat there, mid-discussion about which three people we would take on a desert island with us, we were interrupted by a bloke at the side of me saying,

'Do you know you've got a possum between your legs?' Bloody hell, that's a bit cheeky I thought, and a bit personal, I shaved this morning. But as I looked down to check I was not showing off my lady garden for all and sundry to admire… Eeek… there really was a possum between my legs. Now if you're not sure what a possum is, it's a sort of big, but cute, ratty looking creature. Although I was a little shocked, I was pretty sure it was not about to maim or kill me in any way, so we just sat watching it, intrigued as it munched away happily on a discarded chip before it simply scurried away to the bins, no doubt looking for his main course of left over fish followed by a half-eaten ice-cream cone for dessert.

The possum incident had however, given the bloke and his mate the ideal opportunity to talk to us; I'm sure it's not a chat up line I'll ever hear again unless I decide to go for the unruly pubic look and wear a skirt the width of a belt. Let's face it though, a skirt short enough to give a glimpse of my undercarriage is not a good look at my age, so unless I run out of money and have to flog my wares on the soggy streets of Manchester, it isn't going to happen. When I used to work in Manchester city centre I'd pass a particularly notorious area for this; you'd see the poor girls out there on a winter's day at 6:30 in the morning still looking for passing trade, skirts up to their bum cheeks with legs so blue that it looked like Father Abraham had taken to pimping his merry band of Smurfs.

Once again, we had seemed to outdo ourselves in the attractiveness of the blokes that we'd managed to pull. Although they both appeared to only be in their late 50s, not bad by our standards, unfortunately that's where the positive comments end. These poor men had clearly been at the back of the queue behind *Mr Bean* when looks were being handed out and, as for their physique, the last time I saw a pair of legs like that they were hanging out of a nest. One of the blokes also had so many tattoos up his arms and neck that he looked like he'd been in close proximity to a blast in an ink factory.

I'm not a fan of tattoos at the best of times, and these days there are so many around it's hard to find somebody without some form of art displayed on their bodies. These range from Chinese symbols, that could mean, 'I'm a gullible twat', to a picture of their pet Chihuahua in a pink tutu. I blame David Beckham for this 'inky trend' but, as this bloke was definitely not a follower of fashion judging by the dog-eared t-shirt, gold chain and Bermuda shorts, I could only assume that he was as rough as a badger's arse.

His mate, who made me feel tall, resembled *ET* in a vest top, as he stood there with his overly suntanned wrinkly body on display. As he started to make small talk with us, it also became apparent that he had a really bad speech impediment. Now, I'm not one to ridicule somebody who is unfortunate enough to have the hardship of being unable to pronounce their words correctly, but as he wittered on about the, 'sssssshhunny weasher' and the, 'Beautiful ssshhhunsssshhhet over the sshheea' I couldn't help but be reminded of Sid the Sloth in *Ice Age*; this bloke spoke EXACTLY the same! I think it was safe to say that I'd excelled myself this time by drawing the unwanted attention of a fella who looked like the little alien with the big 'phone bill and sounded like the annoying sloth with a verbal impairment.

'Sid', as I'll call him, lived on the island and had the job of maintaining the gardens of the apartment complexes, hence the skin resembling the texture of a month-old dried peach. What is it with me and gardeners? His tattooed mate was just out visiting him and, despite Sid waxing lyrically about the beauty of the island, I got the impression that he was a lonely soul. My theory was confirmed when he confessed, after only ten minutes in my company, that he was looking for somebody just like me to share his life. Christ on a bike, this poor bloke not only had unfortunate looks and a speech impediment to contend with, but he was also clearly insane. That's what too much sun does for you.

We eventually made our escape with the excuse that we'd a meal booked and we wanted to get an early night due to having to be up at the crack of dawn the next day to go snorkelling. This was partial bullshit of course as, although we were going snorkelling, we didn't really want an early night, but it did the trick. We then spent the rest of the holiday avoiding any gardens where there could be an extra-terrestrial tending to the foliage.

14

Sea Legs and Sea Creatures

I awoke the following morning, after a hot and restless night, with yet another thick head and hair that looked like it had been in the tumble dryer and then repeatedly stamped on with a sweaty boot. A very attractive look.

Although the air-conditioning was great it only had two options: freeze to death in a noisy icy blast, or off. I had therefore spent the night switching between the two. The bed sheets were like the covers at Wimbledon on a rainy day…covers on …covers off…covers on…covers off as I went from sweating to freezing a number of times.

Having dragged ourselves out of bed early in preparation for our snorkelling adventure, we were extremely disappointed to receive a call to say that it had been cancelled due to the choppy conditions. Choppy? What on earth were they talking about? From our balcony, it looked like the picture of serenity, with just an odd white ripple to disrupt the glassy blue waters. The wimpy buggers had obviously never been sat on a freezing cold beach in Wales trying to stem the onslaught of the waves like King Canute, or we'd be still hitting the high seas with a dose of Sea-legs and sick bag.

Still, we wanted the experience to be worthwhile and we were at least able to re-book for the next morning, when hopefully the conditions would mean that I didn't arrive at our destination with my morning breakfast strewn across the boat, or worse still stuck in the hair of one of my fellow snorkelers. I'm the woman that performed a multi-coloured yawn after only half an hour on a pedalo and caused a teacup ride at Alton Towers to be abandoned after a bad experience involving a regurgitated chocolate milkshake and a two-year-old boy who ended up wearing it… and no it wasn't my child. I'm fine on the big adrenalin fuelled fast rides that make your heart race and test out your bladder control, but put me on one of the ones that involve any form of slow repetitive motion and I'll willingly give up the contents of my stomach on anybody sat within vomiting distance.

As we'd now got most of the day to spare, we decided to just relax on the beach. This would have been a great plan were it not for the fact that, by the time we got there, the weather at best could be described as tropical, but more realistically was just downright hot and sticky with a bit of clamminess thrown in for good measure. The humidity levels seemed to hit an all-time high so that merely getting in and out of the golf buggy caused sweat to seep from every pore; some of which I didn't know I had. You know when you get that really awful feeling when you're so hot you can feel small trickles of water running between your boobs? This is what I refer to as titty creek. However, I was so hot that the sweat oozing between my breasts had now developed into a titty river which was flowing all the way down to fanny falls.

We'd come prepared for our relaxing trip to the beach with the obligatory beach towel, sun cream, bottles of water and reading material. We were now ready to lie there and do nothing more strenuous than applying a coat of sun cream and flick the page turner on the Kindle.

The weather, however, had different ideas as the wind whipped up to almost gale-force magnitude. Being British, and not wanting to be beaten by something as menial as a gust of wind, we ensued on a battle of epic proportions, trying to get the beach towels down without being either flogged or mummified. Maybe the snorkelling company had been right to postpone looking at the rough ocean waters that had replaced the crystal-clear mill pond. In the end though, even we had to concede the ridiculousness of sitting there being sandblasted. There was only one thing for it: cocktails!

There's nothing better than being on holiday where you can start on the cocktails at the most ridiculous time of day as all drinking rules that we set ourselves at home go out the window. Can you imagine being at home on a Sunday thinking, *Hmmmm, the weather looks a bit drab, let's go and have a cocktail*? It just doesn't happen. Being away from it all means that you don't have the same mental constraints when it comes to drinking highly potent concoctions of alcohol and fruit juice at lunch time; you can even consider it as one of your five-a-day, I reckon.

Having packed away the sandy towels and exfoliated ourselves removing the grit, we found a really nice bar at the local hotel where we could sit in the pool while we drank. I love these aquatic bars; it means you can stay relatively cool when the unbearable heat and humidity would enable you to poach an egg in your cleavage but, as your bottom half is submerged in the water, all it takes to cool the top half is a graceful dip. You would never be able to, or want to, do this at home. Can imagine the scene at the local public baths? The smell of a mixture of chlorine and the disinfectant foot wells wafting up your nostrils, as you sit at the bar next to a little old lady, who only came in for an orthopaedic swim class to improve her posture after a hip replacement, and is now telling you all about her ailments whilst sipping a Slippery Nipple.

Cocktails in the day are all well and good, but what this does mean is that your judgement is not always at its greatest when deciding how to then spend the evening. By the time we emerged from the bar, a bit on the tiddly side, the weather had calmed considerably, so as we meandered past the harbour area we decided in a moment of cocktail-fuelled madness that we'd book a sunset catamaran cruise for that very evening.

Remember me saying earlier how boats are not really my thing? Well, after consuming copious amounts of alcohol, this was apparently not a factor that my brain could comprehend, and so it merrily chose to ignore the fact that I had drunk lots, eaten less and now I was about to embark on a vessel that looked about as stable as Humpty Dumpty sitting on his wall after a pint of eggnog.

I'd never been on a catamaran before, but having the reasoning capability of a whisky-filled grain weevil, we thought nothing of venturing to the front of the boat to perch ourselves in the prime spot. This did however, involve climbing over fairly wobbly netting, not an easy task at the best of times but even more hazardous when your balance is impaired by copious amounts of alcohol and ill-fitting flip-flops. Even the most skilled *Cirque de Solei* trapeze artist would've found this task a challenge, but for two clumsy tiddly women it meant that we had to practically crawl on our hands and knees to reach our destination.

Having managed to park our backsides on the netting, with the grace of a couple of floundering trout, we were then given a short safety briefing followed by…champagne! Dear God, one thing we did not need was more alcohol but, never ones to refuse a glass of bubbly, we nonetheless gratefully accepted.

The catamaran set sail into the beautiful ocean; the sea was calm, the breeze was cooling and the champagne was going down very well. All was going too smoothly, there was no sea sickness, no incidents of falling overboard, the sunset was exceptionally stunning and the drink just kept flowing.

We returned to the harbour, having thoroughly enjoyed the trip and feeling ever so slightly inebriated, okay, completely rat-arsed. As I disembarked from the boat, my legs had a different agenda to the one my brain had set for them, and decided that they no longer wanted to co-operate with the rest of my body...or each other! With the additional handicap of flip-flops, it looked like an edition of *Total Wipeout;* which is exactly what I did to the poor woman in front as I caught my flip-flop in the netting and propelled forward onto her as I unsuccessfully tried to steady myself. Don't worry, she didn't go overboard as fortunately her rotund husband was on hand to break the fall; I don't understand German but I'm pretty sure the words, 'Fucking Dummkopf' that he muttered, means the same in any language.

The following day, we set off early for our next boating adventure with slightly woolly heads. Being sozzled the night before was not the best preparation given my tendencies to empty the contents of my stomach at the merest bob... I mean the boat bobbing, I don't throw up over any bloke named Robert! I needn't have worried though as there was certainly no bobbing on this trip.

Having glided over the calm waters of the sheltered bay with little more than a dip, it was then time to hit the not so sheltered bit. Christ on a Cruiser…it was full-on rollercoaster time! We're not even talking about a bit of up and down here, no, that could have been fun. Try to think about the biggest roller coaster you have ever been on, and combine that with the Wild Mouse ride. I know the Wild Mouse doesn't sound particularly terrifying, but if you've ever been on this little jewel of an adrenaline ride, you'll know exactly what I mean. You're sat (not strapped) in a carriage the size of a roller skate with a small loosely-fitting wobbly bar across your midriff for safety. You're then catapulted up and down the rails and into the hairpin corners at terrifying speeds, optimising the sensation that you're about to be launched into mid-air with the audaciousness of Evel Knievel. The chances of you not coming off the ride with a severe case of whiplash or a bruised hip bone are frankly non-existent, unless you have a neck like Mike Tyson or so much padding round your arse you'll look like you are sporting a nappy.

So, as we hit the open seas the waves grew bigger and bigger; in fact I would go as far as to say they were frigging MASSIVE! Thank God they cancelled the day before if this was what calm looked like. On the plus side, my head had miraculously cleared, and I didn't even think about feeling sick once. That's because I was too terrified; fear gripped me with every bump and bounce as the bottom of the speedboat thudded over the waves and lurched into the abyss below. I can't say that my anxieties were quelled much by the constant whooping and hollering of the clearly insane lunatic driving the boat either. This was obviously how he got his thrills from an otherwise mundane existence, as no amount of crying and wailing from unsuspecting tourists, was going to impinge on his enjoyment.

Eventually, we hit calmer waters as we approached our destination for the snorkelling. I'm sure the view would have been stunning were it not for the fact that the salty tears and seawater were combining to blur my vision more than the night before. I couldn't even wipe my eyes, as this would have meant releasing my vice-like grip from the rail in front of me. Had my hands been superglued they would have been easier to release. I was not alone in feeling that this had been a ride of terrifying magnitude. As I looked around the boat to see one woman crying hysterically with what looked like a pot of Vic thrown across her face as tears streamed from her eyes and trails of glistening mucus were strewn across her cheeks; not a photo for the holiday album I felt.

Having moored the boat in the shallow waters, we disembarked with shaky legs and paddled the short distance to the beach. It was stunningly beautiful and as I'd imagined with clear blue waters and fine sugary sand. We were each given a wetsuit, flippers and snorkel; the wetsuit was required as at this time of year the oceans were visited by box jellyfish which were extremely poisonous should they sting your naked skin. Great, another dangerous creature to avoid. As if being on the lookout for a stray shark wasn't enough, I now had to keep a keen eye out for scary looking blobs that may be floating by. At this point I asked myself why in God's name I decided to go snorkelling, as the thoughts of being surrounded by fish whilst being submerged under the water was not one that filled me with joy. Everybody kept telling me that you can't go to the Great Barrier Reef and not go snorkelling, so here I was, a virgin snorkeller flipping my way into the water with much trepidation.

After the limited instructions on how to snorkel were given: 'Breathe through your mouth and just swim', we were ready to go. Health and safety were obviously not of paramount concern in this part of the world, with just a basic safety instruction of, 'Don't stray too far from the boat and holler if you get stuck.' *Oh don't worry mate. I'll be sticking close by and you'd hear me from the mainland if I come across anything remotely dangerous.*

I'd thought that my fear would first materialise at the sign of a hoard of scaly little blighters swarming around me ready to nibble on my extremities, but actually my first panic attack came was when I submerged my face in the water and tried to breathe through the mouthpiece of the snorkel. Now this may sound a bit odd to you normal people who've never tried snorkelling. Surely breathing through your mouth is not an act that requires much thought or skill, but place a plastic tube in there and plunge your head beneath the waves and all I could do was breathe through my nose or not breathe at all! It MAY have helped to stop talking too, but as I gurgled the words, 'I can't bloody breathe,' I flailed and splashed around like a harpooned whale in about a foot of water.

I eventually calmed down and started to breathe through the snorkel properly after being encouraged so eloquently by Em as she laughed at my attempt to impersonate Orca.

'You daft sod, stop bloody talking and hold your nose if it's too difficult to not breathe through it.' I sounded just like Darth Vader as I tentatively edged myself a little bit deeper so that there was a chance of seeing some fish rather than just a stray flip-flop that somebody had left too close to the shore. It was amazing and strangely enough I didn't feel threatened by the colourful and slightly nosy little Nemos that swum around me inquisitively. I did have one slight heart-fluttering moment when I thought I saw a tiny jelly fish, but it merely turned out to be somebody's phlegm floating by.

The time actually went a little bit too quickly, having spent half of it trying to get the hang of breathing. Since returning home, and admitting this quirky inability to breathe through a snorkel, I've been surprised how many people have said they were the same so, my advice to anybody planning to partake in this activity, is to have a practice in the bath beforehand. This may seem a bit odd, and admittedly you'd look a total idiot lying there, belly down, in the bath with a snorkel on, but who's going to know and it could definitely save you the embarrassment of looking like a total buffoon as you splash and choke in front of a group of onlookers. You never know, you may find that you enjoy having a bath with a snorkel on, but perhaps warn any prospective bath buddy if it's dangling from your bath tap. There's nothing more likely to convince any partner that you're a total freak than thinking you'll be ogling his tackle through the bubbles as you go for the deep dive.

After the snorkelling adventure and an unsuccessful search for the hysterical woman's missing flip-flop - she was not having a good day - we made our way over to Whitehaven beach. This is supposed to be one of the most beautiful beaches in the world with miles of gorgeous, fine white powdery sand and crystal-clear waters. Unfortunately, due to a recent storm the beach looked more like Whitehaven beach in Cumbria with seaweed, twigs and other debris strewn across it. The clouds had also descended making the grey and murky picture complete. The only things missing in the comparison with its Lakeland namesake, were the smell of fish and chips, aggressive seagulls and some fat woman in a dodgy wig sat on a mobility scooter shouting, 'Get out the fucking way'. It's such a shame as it has a beautiful harbour and stunning views of the coastline, but like many other seaside places in Britain, there has been an obvious decline in their main industries and, along with the inclement British weather, this means that instead of attracting the millionaires to invest a fortune on ocean view apartments and swanky restaurants, you get council run B&Bs, pound shops galore and yet another Greggs.

Having spent a couple of hours sat on the seaweed, watching the clouds building ominously overhead, it was time for the dreaded boat trip back. The hysterical woman was being coaxed aboard in her one flip-flop, whist she jabbered away about not wanting to get on and asking whether there was an alternative way back. At least this time we were prepared for the heart-thumping experience, and the adrenalin-fuelled driver had also decided that, in order to preserve his employed status, he'd best take it a little easier. It was still a very choppy and slightly scary trip back, but at least I managed to keep the contents of my stomach where they should be.

By the time we got back to the harbour I reflected that all in all it had been an enjoyable, although mildly petrifying, trip out. I'm not sure that the hysterical one flip-flopped woman thought the same mind you, I don't think she will be entertaining another boat trip any time soon.

15

Tears and Tribulations

For our final full day on the island we'd planned a trip to a little nature reserve to see the native species of Australia, followed by an afternoon trip to the spa, not to be mistaken with the Spar I once put in an email … a pint of milk, a scratch card and a facial please.

After begging and pleading with Em to let me drive the buggy, she finally succumbed saying I could drive the short distance to the nature reserve. This five minute drive actually ended up taking more like twenty having first caused a buggy jam whilst attempting a ten-point turn manoeuvre to get on the right road. I then stalled and couldn't get it started again; it was at this point Em decided enough was enough and took over control with the impatience of a parent teaching their child to drive.

The nature reserve was really lovely with all the animals you would expect to see associated with Australia ranging from the dangerous to the adorable. The koalas were the cutest though and we just couldn't resist having our picture taken holding one. Now I know for anybody reading this who doesn't agree with either zoos or keeping animals in captivity, this doesn't seem in keeping with the whole ethos of conservation, and with some animals and institutions I whole heartedly agree. Snakes that are passed around willy- nilly with no care for how they're handled, or bears that are trained to dance by making them walk on hot coals appal me, and I would never condone or encourage this is any way. This nature reserve, however, ploughed all the money made back into either conservation work or maintaining the small reserve that was home to these few animals that had been rescued and couldn't go back into the wild even if they wanted to.

The experience with the koalas was restricted to only a small number of people and you were instructed on how to hold them first, as well as only being allowed to do so with the handler stood by. Let's face it too, koalas aren't exactly the most active animal; they sleep 20 hours a day and for the other four they just get chilled out on eucalyptus leaves with an occasional s-l-o-w walk to the next branch where they go to sleep again. Unfortunately, Kevin, the less than docile Koala that I was holding had other ideas, as the randy little bugger kept grabbing my boob. Despite the removal of his paw by the smirking handler, back it kept going for another grope. The photo ended up looking like koala porn!

After a light lunch, and a couple of cocktails, it was then time for our spa treatment: an anti-ageing facial (well a girl needs all the help she can get) and a relaxing back massage. As Em emerged from her session, she had a look of one of the drowsy koalas we'd seen earlier with droopy eyes and a 'who turned the bloody light on' expression. However, she also seemed to be sporting what seemed to be an unravelled wicker basket on her head; not her best look I felt but very amusing to her cruel friend.

My adventure down under was now nearly at an end, with just one more night to be spent in Sydney before catching my flight home. As you can imagine the mood had dropped somewhat with my impending departure, which was not helped by the incessant rain. I see pictures galore of the iconic Sydney Bridge and Opera House bathed in glorious sunshine against a backdrop of clear blue skies with tourists pictured in shorts and t-shirts with big toothy smiles on their faces at the sheer enjoyment and wonder of the beautiful sights. When I was there it looked more like Salford Quays on a drab grey day with a load of miserable looking people huddled together clad in those see-through ponchos that make you look like a giant sperm.

It was a shame really, as the following day was due to be the climax to the month-long Mardi Gras with a big parade through the centre of Sydney culminating in lots of gregarious floats and numerous outdoor events. Well it is Australia, surely you can guarantee the weather? Clearly not. I've never seen so many soaked drag queens sporting makeup like Alice Cooper and feather boas looking more like a mauled, swallowed and regurgitated canary than the light colourful plumage of an exotic bird of paradise.

It certainly made for an interesting last night for people-watching as we sat in Darling Harbour having our final sumptuous meal whilst enjoying the last bottle of Pinot before I began a serious detox on my return home. I'm sure my liver must have been doing somersaults at the thoughts of not having to work so hard to process the daily swamping of alcohol it had needed to contend with for the past couple of weeks.

The trip to the airport the following day was a quiet one, however, the inevitable tears were completely unavoidable as we said our goodbyes at the drop off point crying like a couple of Oscar winning actresses. Eat your heart out Kate Winslet. So, it was with red eyes and a blotchy face that I approached the check-in desk to once again get questioned about being Mr Parkes. Well it was the Mardi Gras after all so I suppose their suspicions were not completely unfounded.

Having passed through security, I sat awaiting my flight reflecting on what a fabulous holiday it had been, whilst again covertly checking out my fellow passengers. Fortunately, when I boarded the plane, I was sat next to a really pleasant elderly lady who'd been visiting her daughter for the last month. In between sleeping and eating we chatted amiably about what we'd been doing with no mention of her love life, ailments, or how many friends had died while she'd been away. The flight…well flew by. Then came the changeover... As we'd been delayed on landing, the two hours I'd originally had for my stop-over had been dramatically cut to about the same time you'd need to hard boil an egg. The minute the transfer bus jerked to an abrupt stop, all the people who were going on to a further destination began to launch themselves through the half-open doors. My God, it was worse than a Take That concert, with people pushing and shoving to get through first. I narrowly avoided being bowled over by a particularly aggressive woman in a pink tracksuit with matching holdall as she railroaded me out of the way like a hostile Mr Blobby.

A quick scan of the boards told me the gate number we'd been given was correct but I'd need to run faster than Usain Bolt if I was to make it. At least this time I wasn't being accompanied by an asthmatic vertically challenged bag of wind, so I could continue my run to the gate unhindered. Judging by the speed of a bloke being pushed in a wheelchair, I was not alone in my mission to get there in record time. The poor fella had a look of a startled rabbit as he was weaved around people at an alarming speed.

Fortunately, I made it through security unhindered, darting out of the other side putting on my belt and shoes quicker than a politician in a brothel raid...I even managed to dash into the empty booze shop to quickly buy the vodka...... well a girl's got to have priorities you know! As I arrived at the gate I could see that people were still boarding and others were still arriving looking just as sweaty and harassed as me. Phew, I'd made it in time: right gate, right flight, right destination.

With much relief, I boarded the plane and flopped into my seat. Great, nobody next to me yet and the window seat was occupied by a young girl with headphones on, so obviously, she was going to be nice and quiet.

As the late arrivals started to board I could see a...hmmm...how shall I word this? A rotund gentleman heading up the aisle. Now when I say heading, I think the term squeezing up the aisle would be more appropriate. One poor child nearly got dragged out of the arms of his unsuspecting mother as his belly swept by in a tsunami of blubber. Good grief, it would be like fitting a rhinoceros into a smart car getting this man into a seat, and I just knew he was heading to the empty one next to me despite my silent pleas of 'please walk past, please walk past'. Yep, as soon as he got to within stomach distance, he stopped... right at the side of me with his enormous belly resting at the same height as my head. I now knew what it must be like to be involved in a car crash with an enormous airbag having just being deployed right into my face.

'Excuse me. I think that's my seat' he said from above his airbag. Yes of course it is. Why wouldn't it be? There's a whole plane of people here but I had a feeling you would be right here next to me.

As I settled down for the long flight I just knew the sodding gods of chance would be partying and laughing about this one for some time to come.

16

The Waiting and Dating Game

I'd been back in the country a couple of weeks and disappointingly I'd had no call or message from Peter, but there again, I hadn't even thought to take his number. When I was young, free and single, and rocking a smaller ass and a flatter belly, it had always been down to the opposite sex to make the first move.

Long before mobiles came into play, any potential relationships had to be played out on the communal landline in the hallway within earshot of the rest of the family. Many an awkward conversation was held freezing my butt off, sat on the bottom stair trying to speak quieter than a church mouse with laryngitis so nobody else could hear. Of course, that's until my Dad would shout, 'Are you still on that bloody phone? I hope they rang you. Do you know how much it costs?' Who said romance died with the onset of age.

These days though, it doesn't seem as daunting to test the relationship waters, as you always have the option to make that initial contact via a text message.

This then gives you the opportunity to write, re-word, delete and try again before hitting that send button.

Mobiles also make it so much easier to keep in touch too. As I've always had a knack of getting lost, a mobile phone would have been an absolute godsend for my parents when I took my first fledgling steps out into the big wide world.

Even when I was at school I had the sense of direction of a stunned turkey, so it will come as no surprise to you that my Mum was on the verge of calling the local constabulary on one occasion when this teenage girl ventured into Manchester.

To be fair to my younger directionally-challenged self, the Arndale Centre, which was the hub of the city centre and where all the spotty adolescents congregated to spend their hard-earned pocket money, was one of the ugliest shopping centres you were likely to clap eyes on outside of Milton Keynes. Whoever had designed the monstrosity must have thought that a shopping arcade resembling a giant public toilet the colour of a dirty dishcloth was the future. They had also been considerate enough to put the bus depot on both sides of the road that ran right through the middle, making it extremely difficult for a couple of distracted teenage girls to identify their bus stop.

What you also need to consider as part of my defence, is that the latest copy of *Smash Hits* had just come out. Not in itself a major event, but as we strolled along engrossed in a particularly hot pull-out of Paul

Young, in a very attractive full denim look that would now sadly be associated more with Jeremy Clarkson than a pop god, we were not really paying attention to where we needed to catch the bus home. Although we ended up on the right number bus, we were going in completely the wrong direction. It was only after half an hour of a world changing debate about who had the fittest arse in tight black jeans, Bono from U2 or Stuart Adamson from Big Country, that we thought to actually look out of the steamed-up window to see where we were: confusion was written across our youthful inattentive faces.

After another five minutes of the usual, 'You ask' 'No, you ask. You're better at it than me,' followed by the only fair way to make major decisions: rock-paper-scissors, we tentatively swayed our way up the aisle from the back to the bus driver.

'Excuse me please,' I said in my politest voice, 'but have we passed Didsbury yet?'

Fortunately, we were stopped at lights at the time as the bus driver couldn't contain his amusement at my innocent question. Through his considerable belly laughs, he cheerfully informed us that we were in North Manchester not south so we'd need to get off the bus, cross over the road and wait for the returning bus on the other side. So, it was with cheeks redder than a couple of Christmas berries that we left the bus and waited patiently on the other side. Fortunately, as the lip gloss I'd been intending to buy wasn't available in the shocking shade of pink that matched my all-in-one jump suit (only in the 80s would that sentence sound right), we had enough money to get home. As the bus pulled up a good half hour later, who do you think the bus driver was? Yes, you've guessed it, the joker who'd laughed his nuts off when telling us we'd need to get off. I'm sure that he had many a chuckle to himself over that little anecdote…GIT.

As you can well imagine, by the time I sheepishly arrived home over two and a half hours late, my Mum was whirling around the hallway like a hyperactive Tasmanian devil, imagining all the bad things that could have happened to her youngest offspring.

'Oh my God! Thank goodness you're back!' she said as she practically bowled me over with a hug that almost crushed the last bit of air out of my already empty lungs after the run from the bus stop.

'Where have you been? I've been worried sick! I've been on the phone all night trying to find where you were!'

As a teenager, I thought this was a tad dramatic for the amount of time I'd been missing, but I guess being a parent now where I worry just as much, that maybe I shouldn't judge too harshly. I know my Dad was equally worried from the look of relief on his face but, having now seen that his beloved daughter was safe and well, and not currently being shipped to the continent as part of the white slave trade, his thoughts turned more to the phone bill that would be dropping through the door as a result of the search.

I think you'll agree that, as this was only one of a few incidents over the years where a mobile phone could have prevented a lot of unnecessary worry for my poor parents, being able to keep in touch with our friends and loved ones, when you're the sort of person who spends much of her time in a location daze, is definitely a good thing. A quick text message to say where I am, or think I am, just means that when I turn up later than Rip Van Winkle for his breakfast, nobody is worried. Although, when I got my first mobile, a quick message was not a concept that could be applied. By the time I'd worked out how many times I had to press the buttons to get a H an E an L another L and an O, a carrier pigeon could have relayed my location quicker.

My speed has improved, however, this is mainly down to the development of predictive text. Although, as you've probably guessed, I've sent an odd inappropriate message in my time. I'm sure you'll all have ones of your own, let's face it we've all done it. My personal favourite, is when I replied to a friend of mine that I was 'Out WANKING the dog'. Obviously, I was not merrily informing him that I had now turned to bestiality; just one wrong letter and the whole meaning of the sentence changed.

However, as I'd not had the foresight to take Peter's number while on the flight, there was no possibility of me sending an appropriate or inappropriate text to say 'Hi'. It was therefore a waiting game to see if he'd contact me, or if he'd disposed of my number along with his plane ticket stubs.

For the first week after returning, every time I got a call from a number I didn't recognise, I would answer in my sexiest voice only to be asked if I was aware about claiming PPI. You would have to have lived on Mars with your head up a Martian's backside for the last five years to have not heard of it. So, by the time Peter did call, just over two weeks after getting back, I practically barked, 'Hello!' down the phone like a Doberman with PMT.

It didn't help that when he rang I was in the process of extracting Ferdinand from a gap under the cupboard where he'd jammed his head in an attempt to get at a piece of his food that had fallen under when I was putting his dinner out. The poor bloke must have thought he'd got the wrong number, as the sweet and pleasant woman he had chatted to on the plane had turned into a female version of Victor Meldrew.

As he stuttered 'Oh…Erm… Hi… I'm not sure if I've got the right number. Is that Isobel?'

Oh no. He's already wondering if he should have called and all I've said is 'Hello'. I quickly tried to rectify my tone.

'Hi. Yeessss it iiiiiiss'

Unfortunately, I said this at the same time as dragging Ferdinand out so all I accomplished was to sound like I was mid-strain of one sort or another. 'Oh. Hi. It's Peter here. We met on the flight to Australia a few weeks ago and you gave me your number. Is now a bad time?'

Having managed to at least control my greedy dog for a second, I hastily explained the situation before he put the phone down quicker that if he'd rung the Scientologists Membership line.

'No, it's fine honestly, it's just that my dog is currently trying to retrieve a morsel of food from under the cupboard in a space the size that an anorexic mouse would struggle with, never mind a slightly chubby cocker spaniel. Just let me sort him out and I'll be with you in a tick'.

He now had to listen to my distant grunts and groans, like some arthritic pensioner attempting the downward dog, as I stretched under the cupboard to retrieve the morsel of dirt-covered food before putting it in the bin, much to the dissatisfaction of my greedy pooch. Surprisingly, he was still on the phone when I'd dusted myself down and managed to assemble something approaching normality in my voice.

'Hi. Sorry about that. How are you?' At least the distraction of listening to noises that could only be heard in *Cocoon 2* the adult movie, had got rid of any tension as he laughed and said, 'Well, better than you from the sounds of it!'

We then chatted about what we'd done while we were away, I obviously missed out the more embarrassing incidents and instead went for the sane version so he didn't think I was an arachnophobic alcoholic with the driving skills of a blind chipmunk. After chatting for a length of time that would have had my Dad pacing up and down the hallway wondering who had rung who, he finally asked the question I'd been hoping for,

'Would you like to meet up for a drink and a meal sometime?'

GOD WOULD I!! Of course, I didn't actually say that, as I didn't want him to think I was more desperate than Desperate Dan at a Hollands pie factory. But, as I hadn't felt like this about any of the men I'd met previously, I wasn't going to pretend I wasn't sure when we'd obviously hit it off twice now.

Next came the decision of where and when, quite important for a first date. You don't want somewhere too quiet that you feel about as conspicuous as Quasimodo at a bell ringer's convention, but I didn't want somewhere so hip and young that somebody would mistakenly think I was there to pick up my son.

After much indecisiveness, we arranged to meet the following Friday at a small pub in the quaint village of Styal that was not too far from either of us. By meeting somewhere I'd have to drive to, I could avoid the evil Pinot powers. A good plan that would ultimately deny my hormones access to my brain, preventing them from taking control to convince my meagre sex deprived mind to do something I could regret, or worse still turn me into a jabbering idiot. It would also ensure that I could get the hell out of there under my own steam if he was either a raging psychopath or a crashing bore who talked about nothing but his ex-wife or cricket. Although there had been no signs of either of these personality traits so far, you just never know.

As I'd been out of the dating game for so long, I got more and more nervous as the date night loomed closer. So much so that I nearly messaged him a number of times to say that I'd been struck down with an extremely rare strain of laryngitis that not only meant that I could no longer speak but also rendered all contact with other people impossible for fear of a nationwide epidemic. This cowardly act was, however, put right out of my head as my ever-astute friend Gill said,

'Don't be so frigging stupid! Get on the date you lunatic.' You can always rely on your friends to boost your confidence and point you in the right direction.

Here's a bit of advice now for anybody finding themselves back in the dating arena after years of gathering dust on the marriage shelf…Never ….and I mean NEVER… look at your naked body in the mirror the night before the date.

For anybody out there who is about to embark on a new relationship after years of taking for granted that the person you're with has seen every bit of your body in all sorts of circumstances, looking at your wobbly bits in a mirror is a definite way to deflate any confidence you may have mustered. As I gazed at my reflection I began to dwell on the fact that where I once had a flat stomach, I now had a slightly flabby one. Where I once had a curvy ass, I now had a cratered one. Where I once had boobs that defied gravity, I now had ones that had given in and said 'bugger that' and gone with the downward momentum.

I also had the dilemma of what to wear … Just when had somebody come into my wardrobe and swapped all the nice vibrant attractive clothes for the frankly colourless ones I saw before me? I was either going to look like I was about to bury somebody, or if I combined the black jeans with the vast array of white tops, I could potentially be asked if I could take the order for table 6. My wardrobe looked like a zebra stood against a piano. The only splash of colour was the orange shoes which were now looking quite appealing, just so he didn't think I was colour blind.

At this point I even considered buying something new the following day, but as I hate shopping and just wouldn't get time, I had to stick with what I owned. I stared at my clothes in desperation hoping that miraculously I would have a Mr Benn moment and I would enter as plain old Izzy and come out as a glamorous woman ready to wow my date. Unfortunately, this was about as likely as the Queen saying to Prince Charles, 'Go on Son, the throne is all yours'.

Friday seemed to be the longest day in history as I worked myself up to the point that laryngitis was once again on the cards… Pull yourself together woman it's a date with a man you've already met, spent hours chatting to and know you like. This is what the little sensible voice in my head kept repeating to me, and although I knew it was true, it didn't stop the hordes of hyperactive butterflies fluttering about mercilessly in my stomach before I left the house.

I arrived at the pub on time and parked up, once again questioning myself. Did I seem too keen or should I have been fashionably late as dating advisors would probably recommend? I didn't really fancy walking into the pub and then having to sit there for ages on my own, looking alternatively at my phone and the door like a nervous meerkat every time somebody came in. I wasn't too concerned that he wouldn't turn up, as he'd messaged me earlier to check I was still okay to meet up and tell me he was looking forward to it. That was a good sign I felt, as he obviously wasn't going down the highly contagious disease excuse.

I needn't have worried about being first there though, as when I walked into the pub he was already stood at the bar, looking about as apprehensive as me. Oh no, what do I do now? Kiss him on the cheek? Hmmm…. maybe a bit too friendly. Shake hands? No…that's a bit too formal. Looking at the strange indecisive expression across his face, he was obviously thinking the same as me. Either that or he had a bad case of wind. There was a slightly awkward moment as I went for the peck and he went for the hand shake resulting in me being stabbed in the stomach and him receiving a peck on the nose, but fortunately all this did was break the ice again as we laughed it off. Thank God for that!

I bet you think I'm going to say now what a disaster it was aren't you? But no, the rest of the evening went really well and flew by as we chatted about music, comedy and anything and everything apart from ex-spouses and cricket. The only awkward moment was when I paid a visit to the ladies' room and on my way back I was asked by a very polite gentleman if I could come and clear their plates for them as they'd been waiting for some time to order coffee. The black jeans and white top combo was the outfit of choice as you may have guessed.

As the evening drew to a close I thought that it was best to call it a night as, although I was as frisky as hell, so could quite easily have invited him back, I didn't want him to think that I was a sex-crazed woman only after one thing.

As we stood in the car park though, we did have a nice kiss accompanied by some very heavy petting that would have been frowned upon at the local baths. It certainly took me back to days gone by when the only place you could get a little bit hands-on was in a secluded place in the local park. Once we'd separated ourselves and come up for air, we decided that next time I would cook him a meal at mine. Brave I know, with my track record in the kitchen. Still, I don't think it was particularly my culinary skills he was after and M&S do make a very good ready meal selection for the incompetent cook.

As I got into my car and drove home I looked like the Joker with a big fat grin and smeared lipstick as a result of the extremely passionate smooch prior to leaving. Christ my bits were flipping more than a pancake-tossing champion.

All I now had to do was not kill him with food poisoning, buy some underwear that didn't look like it was something my granny would wear, and I maybe I'd be in with a chance of some bedroom shenanigans… Oh shit!!!

17

Orville CAN Fly!!

Before I was due to meet up with Peter again though, I just had one small adventure to get through unscathed. Well, when I say small, what I actually mean is high.

With my lust to experience new things in life, I had also inexplicably developed a yearning to do ridiculously adrenalin-fuelled activities that I'd never considered before. The pesky hormones rampaging through my body had obviously convinced my meagre and easily influenced little brain cells that I was now invincible and therefore would be perfectly safe careering through the skies at 100 miles per hour tied to a big sheet and a fat bloke. Yes, this accident-prone chump had willingly signed herself up for a tandem skydive from 10,000 feet!

This madness actually started when I threw myself off a mountain in Turkey on the last holiday before my separation. Don't get me wrong, things had not got so bad that I thought the only option was to end it all in a final swan dive from a great height, but with the temporary insanity of not knowing what was happening in my life, I also lost all rational thinking in wanting to do something that made me feel alive. Strange then, I know, that I thought that throwing myself off the edge of a cliff with a random Turkish bloke would do the trick. It was, however, one of the most exhilarating things I had ever done.

Although my Turkish jump buddy spoke very limited English, and had a squinty eye with a mind of its own that seemed to spasm randomly to one side every time he smiled, he still managed to convey the need to run and jump off the mountain in a miming act that Marcel Marceau would have been proud of. I wasn't sure which way he was looking to indicate where we would be running, but as I was strapped in front of him I was guessing I would know the way to head. The big clue was also the fact that we were going over the edge.

All I could think of as I stood there on legs that were now made of something less stable than jelly, was... Has my brain been possessed by Bear Grylls? ...Is my visually impaired jump buddy able to see where to land? Are we going to end up plunging into the sea if the wonky eye is in control? Unfortunately, no amount of digging my heels in or protesting like a woman on her way to the gallows was going to prevent us from careering towards the edge. I don't think his vocabulary extended to, 'Oh, crap. Can I change my mind?' I remember the words now as I plummeted over the side like a screaming banshee strapped to a Turkish Marty

Feldman lookalike... I will not expand too much but I'm sure you can guess that they contained the words 'Almighty,' 'Christ' and a number of other expletives. However, once we hit the thermals and my stomach made the return journey from my mouth to its rightful position, it was AMAZING. As we floated gracefully through the sky I looked at the breath-taking views below me: mountain ranges, forests, beaches and the aquamarine sea. It was like a picture postcard... WOW!! And I survived... Double WOW!!

The feeling of euphoria and wonder, however, was inevitably replaced by nausea. As you know, I'm not the best when it comes to the contents of my stomach staying firmly where they belong so, as we floated around catching the thermals that send you up and down like a dinghy in a force 9 gale, I began to feel really sick. Oh my God, I now felt worse than I had on the teacup ride! I had to use all my concentration not to pebbledash my meagre breakfast on some poor unsuspecting soul who lay on the beach taking in the rays. Unfortunately, Marty, as I will call him as I never got his name, was either not understanding or not getting it as I tried to convey by the art of mime that I felt sick. I would have thought it was universally known that the motion of retching and covering your mouth signalled that you were somehow feeling queasy. Marty, however, didn't understand or thought it would be fun to just carry on. The final straw came when my flying companion decided to do a nifty little manoeuvre that has only been seen in Bond films, circling at high speed in a spiralled decent. He did regret this however, as the coffee and bread roll made an appearance directly into the lens of his GoPro. That was one video footage that he would not be selling any time soon.

Despite now being dubbed the 'Puking Parachutist', this did not deter me from wanting to feel that adrenalin rush again; I was hooked. So, a few months later, I decided that the only thing for it was to book a tandem skydive. All I needed now was an equally insane jump buddy to share this madcap experience with me. Unsurprisingly most responses to, 'Do you fancy doing a tandem skydive with me?' were met with, 'Are you mad?' 'What the fuck!' 'You barmy cow, you must be joking' or just plain, 'No bloody chance'.

It never even crossed my mind when I was cajoling and unsuccessfully attempting to persuade all my close friends, that I could ask my son, Adam. When I told him what I was intending to do though, he immediately said, 'Amazing, I'll do it with you'. Oh No! Did I really want him doing this with me? What if there was an accident? I would then be responsible for killing or injuring my only child. It was one thing throwing myself out of a plane like a kamikaze muppet, but watching my child do it was another thing altogether. I was hoping that the price of the jump would put him off, or that there would be some unwritten rule about family members jumping together, but no amount of saying, 'Are you sure?' would deter him from accompanying me. Some mothers and sons have nice days out shopping or lunching but, now I had evolved into an adrenaline junkie, we were going to be plummeting through the skies together. In the end, I also managed to rope in an equally willing friend into joining us by using the added incentive that we'd be able to raise some much-needed funds for a local cancer charity. Well, when I say willing, what I really mean is pissed. NEVER EVER agree to something like this after a couple of bottles of wine or the bugger you're drinking with will record it and then hold you to it the next morning.

So, there we have it; Adam, Phil and I were all signed up, and geared up to do a tandem skydive from 10,000 feet, taking off from a tiny airfield in Shropshire. What were we thinking?

By the time D-Day arrived we'd managed to raise a whopping £1,700 in sponsor money between us, so backing out was certainly not an option, unless we wanted to be as popular as Arthur Fowler after he stole the Christmas Club money. The weather conditions on the day could be considered at best, a tad breezy, and at worst, gale force! This was not looking good for our prospects of getting the jump done, but still, we drove to the airfield with a mixture of fear, excitement and trepidation about what the day would hold. Phil had even packed a spare pair of trousers and Calvin Klein's; he said it was just in case he got muddy but I think we knew the real reason.

As we arrived at the waste ground that was masquerading as an airfield, the nerves really started to kick in; unfortunately so did the wind speed. There seemed to be a few people milling about sticking objects and fingers into the air so I was guessing this is how they determined if the conditions were suitable for jumping. This did not bode well.

We made our way nervously to the small hut that doubled as a stomach-churning café and briefing room. The smell of greasy sausage and bacon wafted up my nostrils as we entered the room, making my stomach lurch in a tidal wave of bile. Having given our names in to the homeless-looking person at the desk, we were told that the jump could be cancelled, but to wait around as the weather may change.

The nerves were palpable as we sat there watching short films of previous lunatics careering through the skies in outfits varying from the ridiculous to the non-existent. Yes, I kid you not, there was a flying elephant, that I'm sure caused some unsuspecting onlookers to do a double take, and a hare-brained fool who could be seen jumping in nothing but a pair of boxers. From the looks of the video it didn't seem like winter when he jumped, but even so, the temperature at 10,000 feet even on the balmiest of summer days would have been ball-shrinkingly cold!

As the waiting continued, emotions fluctuated from feeling reprieved that we'd live another day if it was cancelled but, having psyched ourselves up, the thoughts of not being able to jump seemed like such a come down...or not as the case may be. Fortunately, the wind died down enough for the guy with his finger in the air to give the go-ahead for the jumps to commence. Phew and fuck were muttered in equal measures!

As we'd got there early, we were allocated to jump in the second group of the day. This meant that once the green light had been given, we heard our names being called almost straight away to go for the all-important briefing. Gulp...this was really happening!

A group of six petrified individuals were all ushered into a little side room where a scary-looking Sergeant Major of a bloke stood there with a clip board and surly expression that said, 'Mess with me at your peril'. There would be no fooling about on his watch; he made Genghis Khan look like a pleasant welcoming chap in comparison. Still, it was a dangerous thing we were about to attempt so we needed to pay attention, as it was not just our lives but our fellow jumpers we would be putting at risk.

He barked the dos and don'ts at us and then randomly selected us to answer questions in a test to check we'd been paying attention. I felt my mouth go dry as it brought back memories of school, waiting my turn to be picked to read or answer a question. I used to be that worried that, when I was eventually selected, I neither knew where we were up to in the book nor heard the question. Determined that I wasn't going to fail, I paid full attention so that when he snapped my question at me I managed to squawk,

'Head back with legs tucked under,' for the position to be in for the jump. He'd told us that one of the main things to remember (apart from if you feel sick you need to puke in your jump suit!) is that when you land you need to lift your legs up. So, having received instructions on just how to do this, next came the test to see if we could manage it while sat on the floor. Easy peasy for a fit athletic woman like me.

Having passed the briefing tests and signed away all rights to blame and claim should anything go wrong, we were then taken to the fitting room to be kitted out, with a chance for one last pee before being zipped into a purple boiler suit that wouldn't have looked out of place on a 1980s Duran Duran video. Not an eye-catching look for a short slim blonde like myself, but an even less flattering one for a six-foot tall bugger like Phil. Add a pair of goggles to the ensemble and the tight-fitting cap he was wearing, and it was like coming face to face with Tinky Winky in a Biggles hat.

The ridiculousness of the outfits did however take our minds momentarily off what we were about to do, but as we stepped into our harnesses the reality did kick in a bit.

Next came the task of being allocated our jump buddies. Would I get some fit athletic looking bloke with tight muscles he could wrap round me in a vice-like hold? Would I hell as like. There was me hoping to get a Jamie Dornan lookalike, when who rocks up but a cross between Orville and Ronnie Corbett. I felt tall and frankly quite fashionable as I looked at the undersized man before me in a luminous green jump suit. I could see him eyeing Phil up as he came over, I'm not quite sure what he was thinking but I bet it went something along the lines of …. 'Thank God I got the skinny blonde and not the purple man mountain'. Visions of the kids' film *Monsters Inc.* flashed through my mind as the little stumpy green fellow stood next to the big purple giant. Admittedly in the film the little green one only has one eye and, fortunately my jump buddy had two and both pointing in the same direction this time, but even so, neither would have looked out of place in a stage adaptation of the *Pixar* movie.

'Hi. I'm Alec,' said the cheery looking luminous sprout before me. 'I'll be making sure that you get down safe today. Don't worry I've got 20 years of experience and I've never lost anybody yet; I've killed a few but always found them after. Ha-ha.'

I should have known by just looking at his outfit that he would be some sort of comedian, but his cheery face, warming smile and outlandish costume had the desired effect of putting me at ease so, as he checked my harness over and went through all the instructions again with me, I began to immediately relax.

Although there were six virgin jumpers quaking in the briefing room, as the plane was the size of a crop duster and we each had a jump buddy, they split us into groups of three meaning that it was just me, Adam and

Phil on our flight. I have to confess that this was so much better than going in the group of six, especially as one of the other women was already showing signs of not really wanting to go through with it as she sat on a bench with her head in her hands shaking like the proverbial shitting dog. I think more than a little encouragement would be needed to get her up in the plane never mind out of it. You don't need that when you're already feeling like you're just about to do the most dangerous and scariest thing you have ever done in your life…Well if you discount the time I had to go home and face my Mum after I got caught out lying about staying at some friends when I was really at an all-night party. I can tell you, there is NOTHING scarier than facing the hurt, disappointment and annoyance of a woman on the change holding a frying pan.

As we made our way with slightly wobbly legs towards our aircraft we discussed the jumping order: the vertically challenged couple, that was me and Orville, would go first. After a few photos outside the plane trying not to look as nervous as a nun at a penguin shoot, we climbed aboard in reverse order of the jump; first in last out.

We all sat on the floor with our jump buddy behind as they secured all the bindings that would keep us tethered to them for the descent. Christ, this was getting so real now as I sat between Orville's legs feeling his buckles digging in my back side…at least I think it was buckles. The plane made its way over the bumpy grass runway, engines straining as it pulled its nervous cargo into the skies. The noise inside the plane was deafening so this meant that as we climbed there was no chance of conversation; the ascent was limited to hand signals only. We looked like the sign language translators at the bottom on the TV, only in our case the nervous looks, flapping and thumbs up made us look a little more like a crazy bunch of escapees from the local asylum for incompetent fashionistas.

As we climbed higher and higher and the clouds became our viewpoint out of the window, the tension kicked in a little, although looking across at Phil I realised that actually in comparison I didn't feel too bad. Maybe the spare undies were a good idea for him. Adam on the other hand was looking remarkably calm, or maybe he just hid it better.

The tap on my shoulder and instructions to pull the goggles down and shuffle across the floor towards the doorway meant that finally we had reached 10,000 feet. Oh! My! God! This was soooooo arse twitchingly real now!!

As the door opened and the icy blast of air filled the plane we shuffled on our backsides looking like we were doing a very odd version of Oops Upside Your Head. I could see nothing in front of me through the doorway but clouds and I didn't dare look down as we reached the edge of the plane. I took one last look back at Adam and half smiled and half grimaced before turning my attention back to what I was about to do..

'Head back, legs under' 'Head back, legs under' 'Head back, legs under' was all I kept saying to myself. I didn't really need to think about the head back thing as there was NO WAY I was going to look down.

'Legs under' 'Legs Under' 'Legs…. Fuuuuu...!!!!' Before I knew it, we were out and falling, all I could see was the ground a very long distance away careering up towards me at a fair old rate. I couldn't breathe we were going so fast. Why could I not breathe? Had my oxygen deprived brain forgotten how to function enough even to relay the message to be able to take any air into my empty lungs? The speed we were dropping was incredible as Orville and I made a rapid descent through the skies. He could bloody fly now couldn't he!! Although I'm sure that it was not that long, we seemed to be dropping for a lifetime before the parachute was deployed and we were jerked upwards in a crotch cutting motion that I'm sure would have resulted in the bloke who'd jumped in just his underpants having his balls ripped from his body, I hope he'd already got kids.

The relief, adrenaline, and finally air, all flowed through me as I began to actually take in that I was now floating at a less alarming speed. Orville's flapping behind me told me that everything was okay and I gave him the thumbs up to say I was fine… except the cold was causing my nose to dribble quicker than my sniffing capacity, and the lack of tissues meant that the only course of action was to swipe it sideways with my gloved hand.

Still, this slight distraction didn't detract from the wonderful sights before me as I got a bird's eye view of the surrounding countryside, the fields, roads, little houses and even tinier cars all looking like a model village on a grand scale. It was absolutely amazing!

As I'd warned Alec that I had the capacity to throw up more than a pregnant woman with chronic morning sickness, he didn't attempt any death defying spins but just gently took us lower and lower pointing out sites in the distance. I don't think he fancied his lovely green suit being splattered with vomit.

We soon got to the point where we had to prepare for the landing as we were so low we could actually see people looking up, camera phones at the ready in case they were able to post something sinister on the internet. It amazes me that people always seem to be on hand to capture random tragedies or miraculous escapes. Half the time they don't even know the people but are just passers-by who happen to be videoing it. They probably go around with the phone permanently recording just in case they can get their 15 minutes of fame.

Anyway, remember me saying lifting my legs up was easy peasy? Well this is the point where I take that statement back. It may be easy when you are sat with your backside firmly planted on the floor, I've done Pilates y'know so I know I can do things like this. However, when you're dangling mid-air strapped to somebody else and gravity is most definitely working against you, it would be easier lifting them out of a pool full of custard in cement wellies.

I could hear Alec now screaming, 'Lift your legs!' as I desperately tried to heave them up to a horizontal position. It was no good, I was using all my exertion and they were still moving less than when I had an epidural.

What was wrong with me? First my brain forgot to tell my lungs to breathe and now it had lost the ability to communicate with my legs that they needed to bleeding pull up and quickly too! It eventually twigged that I would need to use my arms to provide a bit of muscle to haul them into a seating position. I can tell you it took all my effort to grab the purple shellsuit around my legs and heave them upwards to prevent them taking the impact of the landing, which was clearly what my adequately padded backside was for.

A graceful landing it was not, as we bumped along the ground coming to an abrupt stop as the parachute caught the wind dragging us back slightly the way we came. Alec was quickly up, pulling me with him, controlling the parachute and stopping us from being dragged along like a couple of ragdolls.

I'd done it…… I'd only gone and bloody done it! I couldn't believe it, I'd jumped out of a plane at 10,000 feet and actually enjoyed it. I was so pleased with myself that I hadn't wimped out or cocked up … Amazing!!

I also didn't need to worry about Adam and Phil landing safely as, despite leaving the plane after me, they were already down and waiting at the side of the field. I think Orville must have taken a detour up there. It was with a mixture of relief, euphoria and adrenaline fuelled giddiness that we greeted each other…well if you discount Phil's not-so-polite question of, 'What the hell's that all over your face?'

We had all survived to tell the tale and felt justifiably proud of ourselves. Adam had absolutely loved it and would do it again… any time. Phil, well Phil swore lots, almost got his balls chopped in half when his parachute opened, and nearly crapped himself in the process. Would he do it again? Would he fuck!

Not just that, but we had all raised a load of money for charity, two swore like Glaswegian dockers, one ended up looking like a snot artist had used her face as a canvas, two loved it and would do it again, one needed to buy new undies and is now in therapy.

18

F Bomb to Sex Bomb

After the weekend of high adrenalin and higher alcohol consumption, my mind now turned to the following weekend when I was due to have my second date with Peter. I wasn't so worried that we wouldn't get on, as we'd been messaging each other like a couple of lovestruck teenagers since we last met, maybe with less acne than our younger counterparts and probably at a quarter of the speed, but with just as much gusto.

We'd progressed past the polite stage, asking what we'd done that day, to the horny stage, saying what we'd like to have done that day. He was funny, clever and made me laugh, which was always a big plus in my book. Despite getting flirty during a little bit of sexting, with more bravado than I actually felt, I was really quite anxious at the thought of being naked in front of somebody. As I stared at my pale wobbly bits in the mirror, I decided the only answer was to a) hope for a power cut b) buy dimmer bulbs or c) pray that he had developed cataracts since I'd last seem him. It had been over 20 years since I'd been with a man other than my husband, so I was bound to be a little bit nervous. Okay… massive understatement there… that's like saying Adolf Hitler was a 'little bit of a dictatorial racist'… I was panicky as hell, as I knew that Getting Jiggy with it was definitely something we both wanted.

I temporarily put aside the thoughts of the inevitable unveiling of the flesh though, as I also had to decide what on earth I was going to serve up for dinner. I didn't want to look like I couldn't cook. Hmm… that's garlic bread off the menu then. But I also wanted to look like I could do more than just turn the oven on.

Why I was bothered about this I don't really know, as it wasn't like he was looking to employ me as his housekeeper. I wasn't expecting to produce something that Greg Wallace could 'stick his face in' (that's good by Greg's standards), but I did at least want to serve a two-course meal that was edible and didn't resemble something you'd find on the roadside at Chernobyl.

I also had to consider the flatulence factor; I didn't think that getting all romantic and intimate only to drop a fart loud enough to cause a spike on the Richter scale was a good thing. This limited my choices to nothing too spicy and no mushy peas! The minute the squished green little buggers hit my stomach I can always feel enough gas being generated to compete with the production from the North Sea. Not that I was likely to serve up fish chips and mushy peas as a romantic first dinner. Although there's nothing wrong with this great British traditional dish, the aroma of fried fish and chip fat was not what I wanted Peter to be greeted with, not to mention the aroma later! So, after spending quite some time deliberating and looking at every recipe book in my possession from Mums Know Best to BBQs Made Easy (I didn't even have a barbecue!), I decided that I would play it safe with a chicken, bacon and pasta dish that I'd made a thousand times, followed by an easy to make cheesecake that required no cooking at all. Perfect menu choice.

Having settled on what culinary delights I'd impress Peter with, that really only left me to dwell on the fact that I'd need to undress in front of a man that so far had only seen the flesh on my hands, neck and face; none of which were particularly on the wobbly side. As I rifled through my underwear collection on the hunt for something that I'd look half decent in, the realisation hit me that I was woefully ill-prepared to be in with a chance of looking remotely alluring. All the knickers and bras had either seen better days or were of the plain and practical variety that you bank on nobody seeing.

The only vaguely sexy item was a very thin red thong that I'd once worn over my jeans for Comic Relief. I remember having to walk around the office with the collection bucket as, apart from the occasional red nose dotted about - one of which was alcohol induced - nobody else had really bothered to get into the spirit, so it rested with me and another girl to wander about dressed like confused prostitutes. Oh, there was one other bloke who'd come in with a pair of old red boxers over his trousers, but as they had a particularly worrying dark patch at the back it was felt that it was not a good move to have him parading round in the previously soiled item for all and sundry to see.

As the thong consisted of a tiny red string at the back that would no doubt be eaten up instantly by my greedy bum cheeks, I decided that the look of an uncooked pork joint was not one that would impress. There was nothing for it but to go and buy something new.

As this was a special occasion I thought that instead of my tried and tested store, where I normally purchase my boring t-shirt bras and everyday knickers, I'd pay a visit to a local underwear boutique going all out with the getting measured and buying something that looked really sexy but classy. I could have returned to Anne Summers as they did have some lovely garments, but after my last embarrassing trip I thought I'd give it a miss and avoid the potential of a repeat performance. Hmm... depending on how things went of course.

A trip there in the future could be on the cards, but maybe to confront him on our first sexual encounter wearing a policewoman's tight rubber outfit brandishing a pair of handcuffs could scare him off just a little.

So, the local intimate shop it was then. I think I felt a bit more comfortable with this too when it came to the measuring of my buns. I've never been measured for a bra before, I've always gone for the looks-okay-and-feels-right method. The thoughts of having some bored young shop assistant, who'd only been drafted in from the homeware department due to the qualified measurer having a funny turn whilst cupping a particularly large lady's bazoomers, didn't fill me with confidence. I haven't got the biggest boobs, so what I have got I need to make the most of. Lift and separate is not really something I need to consider ...more like lift and squash up to try and make a cleavage. There again some of the bras these days have that much padding and uplift that you could con a bloke into thinking he was getting to grips with a couple of Whoppers, only to find out later that they'd been replaced by a couple of soggy Egg McMuffins.

I entered the boutique to the sound of a tinkling bell and the smell of overpowering lavender that was somehow being pumped through the vents in a cloud of floral freshness. It was that strong, I'd be lucky if I made it further than the threshold before collapsing into a lavender-induced coma.

I'd been enticed in by the window display that, although limited, did have a couple of nice frilly sets that the more mature and classy lady would wear. No crotchless knickers or rubber peek-a-boo bras in here I thought...and yes, I was right... there were certainly no such kinky garments to be perused or purchased either. Unfortunately, the underwear seemed to be limited, very limited to the couple of items in the window as I stared round at the range of girdles, bolder holders and knickers big enough to be used as the wicket cover at Old Trafford cricket ground. Still, I was in there now, and the bell had announced my arrival, so there was no quick exit from the hawk-like woman now watching me intently from the other side of the counter. Despite giving her what I considered to be a nice smile, her expression remained fixed, looking like she'd just been under the counter licking a battery before I'd had the audacity to walk into her shop and disturb her.

Although I didn't really think she had anything that would suit me, being under the age of 80 and not having boobs that would need a bra the size of two wheelbarrows to keep them from dragging on the floor, I continued to examine what was on display, whilst holding my breath. There seemed to be nothing smaller than a 38DD and there was certainly nothing made with anything resembling lace, with industrial strength double elasticated hold-all-in material being the only option. The parachute for the skydive had been flimsier than the material used for some of the garments in there, but to be fair, your wobbly bits would be wobbling no more having being constrained in something that Houdini himself would struggle getting out of. And get this…I even spotted a rack selling American Tan tights!! Good God! Do you remember them? I think they were supposed to give your legs the illusion of a sun-kissed glow that could only be achieved by bathing in California rays, when in reality they looked more like you'd been dipped in Cuprinol and wrapped in thick nylon. There may still be a market for an armed robber looking to disguise himself as John Merrick with a fake tan, but other than that I can't see her getting rid of her stock any time soon.

So, as I made my way round, with Hawkeye looking at me like something she'd found on the end of her toilet brush, I decided that I could hold my breath no longer, as I'd certainly seen enough to know that I would either need to be at least 40 years older or mental enough to think that looking like *Mrs Doubtfire* on our night of passion would be a good idea. I'm pretty certain too that stripping off to reveal underwear made out of the same material as trampolines would result in the passion draining away quicker than if I told him I had leprosy.

As I made my escape, once again to the sound of the tinkling bell, I gulped in the fresh air filling my now empty lungs before they went into lavender failure. I'd politely nodded a thank you as I left but got nothing but the blank expression back; she hadn't said a word throughout the whole time I'd been in there. Not a 'Can I help you?' 'Is there something specific you're looking for?' not even a 'What on earth are you doing in a shop for the chronically obese or over 80s?' I don't think I'll be putting her forward for Sales Person of the Year. There was more chance of the local butcher getting his hands on my boobs to measure them too. I had a feeling that any measuring she'd do would be a similar experience to having a mammogram. God, how painful are they? It may be a necessary procedure, but I remember the first time I had one. I nervously stood in a freezing cold portacabin in the local surgery carpark having the life pummelled out of my boobs by some vice-like machine that squashed them flat, then vertical, and then continued to squash them until I thought they would burst at the nipple.

Christ almighty does it REALLY have to crush them that hard? Can it not just take a nice little picture without first kneading them mercilessly like an over-enthusiastic teenager or something on the *Great British Bake Off*? Mind you I can't even see Paul Hollywood punishing a bit of dough the way that the mammogram machine treats boobs.

Needless to say, after venturing into the time zone that was boutique shopping, I ultimately decided to return to my usual store and go with the tried and tested looks-okay-and-feels-good method, opting for a nice black lacy bra with matching briefs that at least covered the areas I thought warranted less attention. I actually felt quite sexy as I looked in the mirror on the night of the date. It's amazing what dim lightbulbs and a large glass of *Pinot Grigio* can do.

By the time Peter was due to arrive, the table was set with the candles lit for the added romantic ambiance, as well as further dim lighting, and all was ready in the kitchen. The cheesecake was made and chilling in the fridge, the pasta sauce was bubbling away nicely, the bottle of wine was chilled (minus a large glass) ... and I was nervous as hell! What was I doing? I'd spent the last year as frisky as a bitch on heat and now the time had come to actually do something about it I was more scared than when I was jumping out of the bloody plane. 'CALM DOWN!' the little voice in my head kept saying, 'What's the worst that can happen?' We both knew we liked each other, and although we'd only had one proper date, life's too short to waste time dithering about, and it's not like I was looking for a lifelong commitment.

When the knock at the door came, sending Ferdinand into a tail spinning frenzy, I had calmed slightly, determined to just enjoy the night and go with the flow. Any tension and awkwardness, was quickly overcome as Peter laughed while fending off the frantic dog bouncing at his genitals. Ferdinand is very friendly and likes nothing better than making new human friends, so it was with as much exuberance as he could muster that he greeted this new person into his home…a guard dog he is not!

Fortunately, Peter liked dogs so was comfortable with the attention he was now receiving from my overexcited bouncing pooch with his lipstick very much on display. It's always slightly embarrassing when dogs get over excited in that region, but given what Peter and I both had on our minds, you can't really blame Ferdinand for being on the same wavelength. Although he would NOT be joining in!

'You look lovely,' Peter eventually managed to say

once he had calmed Ferdinand down enough to speak, 'and the food smells great. Did you cook it?' He then smiled his cheeky grin and all the nervousness I'd been feeling seemed to evaporate.

The meal actually turned out quite well, if you ignore the slightly gloopy pasta that I overcooked due to a particularly extensive smooch while it was cooking. Boy, this man could kiss! Also, when I say meal, what I mean is the one course, as the cheesecake I had so lovingly prepared actually didn't make it out of the fridge as the kisses took on a much more passionate nature while we stood in the tiny kitchen.

Peter is quite a bit taller than I am, especially as I had no heels on, so as he lifted me up onto the kitchen top, narrowly avoiding putting my arse in the sink, I wrapped my arms around him and kissed him so he was in no doubt that I couldn't wait to get him in my bed. Bollocks to worrying about being naked, I wanted this man and I wanted him now.

Having come up for air like a couple of asthmatic scuba divers, we disentangled ourselves from an embrace that had wiped the kitchen top clean with my backside and looked knowingly at each other. I took Peter by the hand and started to lead him towards the stairs shimmying as sexily as I could when you have pasta sauce on your arse...HOLY MOLY! I was actually going to make love to this man!

It's at this point when Ferdinand thought that he was also invited to get in on the act as he tried to follow us up the stairs. I don't let him in my bedroom as a rule, and he always sleeps downstairs, so quite why he thought he could come up on this occasion was beyond me. A little bit of protectiveness mixed with not wanting to be left out meant that he now started to cry and howl as I shut the door,,,Good lord you'd have thought I was leaving him alone with Barbara Woodhouse and a chained pit bull the way he was creating!

'You go on up, I'll just give him a dog chew to settle him down and then I'll be right up,' I said as we kissed once more on the stairs. I could have done with that bone little Cedric had been chomping on to keep him occupied. Having found the biggest chew I could, stuffing it with chicken to prolong the chewing time, I made my way upstairs now with a little apprehension. Would he be naked in my bed? Shit! That means he'd be able to watch me undress; getting in between the sheets fully clothed would seem a bit weird. Phew …. As I went in the bedroom he was just sat at the end of the bed looking very sexy, very horny and fortunately, fully clothed. I put on the local radio station, just in case the neighbour was in; I didn't want him telling Sweary Mary about the noises next door for her then to tell the whole neighbourhood that the 'Slapper at number 17 was shagging last night.'

Fortunately, the radio station of choice seemed to be playing mellow music that would blend into the background, not detracting from the sexual tension that had been building to skyscraper heights all night. I couldn't remember feeling this turned on in a long time as we removed each other's clothes slowly kissing and taking in every bit of our newly revealed flesh. His body was not what you could call tanned and, despite his recent trip, his skin was white against the dark hair on his chest as I ran my fingers down his naked torso towards his now unbuckled trousers. He slowly unzipped my dress and let it fall to the floor, 'Oh my God you are so sexy'… Kerching! The underwear and dim bulbs paid off…or maybe he does have cataracts. Either way he thought I looked alluring so my confidence did a little leap of joy.

The intensity of the lust we were feeling as we looked into each other's eyes was quite something as my bits did more summersaults than an Olympic gymnast. We were both totally engrossed in the moment as we lay down on the bed with every inch of me wanting to feel his touch as his hands explored my body gently caressing me and working his hands down towards my ……

'Woof….Whine…whine….whine…….Yap yap…Woof……Whine…whine…whine……yap yap…Woof… Whine whine whine'.

Aaarrggggh…. Having managed to work out how to retrieve the chicken quicker than a contestant on *Brainbox Challenge*, Ferdinand had now started to whine and cry downstairs like an abused dog.

I desperately tried to block out the commotion and concentrate on the feelings of sheer pleasure that were tingling through my entire body. I was sure that if I ignored him he'd go quiet after a short while, but no, the little bugger had different ideas getting louder and louder to the point that all I could hear were his yaps and barks interspersed with snippets of Phyllis Nelson on the radio asking us to Move Closer. There was nothing for it, I would have to do something before Sweary Mary hit her speed dial through to the RSPCA.

'I'm so sorry I don't know what's up with him,' I said breathlessly as I reluctantly peeled myself away from him. 'I'll just go and sort him out …then I'll come back and sort you out,' I joked. Bloody hell! What did I say that for? He'll think he's in a version of *Carry on Bonking*.

To be honest, it's a bit of a passion killer having to stop mid-fumble to go and stuff more chicken in a dog chew than Nandos sell in a month. However, that's exactly what was required as I tried to hide my nakedness, quickly darting downstairs to jam the chew so full that it would be easier to extract coal from a mine shaft with a blunt teaspoon.

Once I was sure that Ferdinand was happily beavering away at his chew like a dog possessed, I went back upstairs quickly diving back in bed before he could see my wobbles. Fortunately, it didn't look like his passion had diminished any as his excitement was obvious as we resumed our passionate embrace to Dr Hook telling us about Sylvia's Mother. I'm not sure I really wanted to know what worldly advice Sylvia's Mother had for me at this point, but I'm guessing it had nothing to do with the thoughts that were running through my mind.

I now felt like I had a whole troop of gymnasts in my nether regions with my bits doing triple cartwheels, back hand springs and 180 split leaps as I continued exploring every inch of him. All I could think of was having this man make love to me. It was at this unfortunate moment that it occurred to me that we'd not even considered or talked about contraception; maybe Sylvia's Mother was getting to me after all!! Oh My God. How could I be so stupid to not even ask?

As I was in the menopause it meant that getting pregnant would probably be about as likely as Oscar Pistorius getting a job at Victoria Bathrooms. Even so, why had I not even given any thought to asking if he had a condom?

'Do you erm…have any protection with you?' I asked both breathlessly and tentatively…The horrified look on his face said it all……

BOLLOCKS!!!

'Oh God no… I just didn't think about it. I've not been with anybody since my relationship ended. I'm sooooo sorry! SHIT!'

This had more of a dampening down on our libidos than if I'd said I had highly infectious genital warts and a dose of the clap. We both sat there on the bed deflated, well emotionally at least, as his protruding manhood was far from deflated, eagerly waggling at me to get my attention blissfully unaware of our dilemma.

'We could do other things and just not have full sex...' Peter said with just a hint of hope in his voice 'It seems a shame to waste this perky little chap when he's got all worked up over your sexy body.'

The combination of the blatant attempt at flattery and, the look that would make a kicked puppy look less helpless, certainly had the desired effect. Hmmm ... 'Other things' did sound quite appealing, given that just the mention of them had set the acrobats into their full routine again sending tingles from my lady parts right the way to my toes. I kissed him gently on the lips and looked once again into those dark gorgeous eyes as I took his still very pert chap gently in my hands...... he was now waggling very excitedly at the prospect of what was to come.

Fortunately, Ferdinand had also finally got the message as not a peep could be heard from downstairs; he had either fallen asleep or had found a way to open the fridge and was now gorging himself on cheesecake.

We were just getting to the climax of our 'other things' when the music took a decidedly strange shift from the romantic warbles of Barry White singing about his first, his last and his everything, to be replaced with, of all things, Gangnam Style. What in the name of all that's Holy just happened? Had somebody crept into the room and changed the radio station while we were engrossed? Nothing is more likely to put you off your stride than trying to orgasm while your brain tries to block out the image of a chunky South Korean bopping up and down like some overweight jockey. For God's sake what is wrong with these radio stations? Do they think that one minute you'd be smooching away all loved-up and horny, and the next you'd be up doing the latest dance craze throwing your arms around in the air and dancing like some lasso wielding line dancer?

We couldn't help but both start laughing at the ridiculousness of the situation. You would think that you couldn't really get a worse song to have sex to after that, wouldn't you? But no, this particular radio station in their wisdom decided that the little fat Korean fellow needed to be followed by two little chirpy Geordie ones. I may like a North Tyneside twang, but I have to draw the line at bonking to PJ and Duncan getting Ready to Rumble!

Having stopped giggling and switched the radio off to silence the Geordie duo mid-rumble, my brain was then able to get back to concentrating on the task in hand…literally. God this 'other things' was damn good stuff as I reached a very satisfying climax that I'm sure rattled my fillings. Peter was also getting to the point of no return, as he let out a groan and an, 'Oh God'. Unfortunately, in his state of ecstasy, his brain seemed to have disengaged the part that was in control of aim and fire. This resulted in what can only be compared to porridge being fired out of a cannon in a high wind.

'Bloody hell,' I giggled,… when we talked about protection I didn't realise that what I actually needed was a pair of goggles and a shower cap!'

I couldn't control my hysteria any longer though, as I tried to resurrect some degree of post-coital euphoria. I had not laughed that hard in ages!

It perhaps wasn't quite the romantic evening I'd planned but, despite the badly timed disruptions from my attention-seeking dog, the lack of contraception and the shagging music that would be better placed at a cheesy disco than a bedroom, it had been one of the most satisfying and funny nights I'd had with any man in a long time. I didn't really feel self-conscious when I was naked, even when I had to fumble my way to the bathroom to unglue my fringe from my forehead… complete with bare arse wobbling behind me.

19

Bunk Beds, Fleeces and Ear Plugs

Although Peter and I were hitting it off spectacularly and having more sex than a prostitute at a political party conference, I still wanted to maintain my new-found independence and look for new ways to meet people who enjoyed the same things as me.

Before I'd embarked on my rampant sex marathon with Peter, I'd booked a weekend away with a walking group that was advertised for the young, and not just the young at heart. The website looked vibrant with pictures of people having a great time walking and partying into the wee small hours; this was not a walking stick and cocoa before bedtime type of walking group. This looked fun.

So, in a moment of madness, yes drunken madness, I booked onto one of their weekend breaks in the Lake District; safe in the knowledge that, should the best entertainment be a talk on waterproofing your boots and the benefits of a decent bobble hat in windy conditions at the top of Crinkle Crags, I could make a hasty retreat back home quicker than you could say fleece knickers.

The accommodation was a youth hostel that was located not too far from Derwent Water at the northern part of the Lake District. Yes, you did read that right: youth bloody hostel!! I'm not necessarily a top end swanky hotel kind of girl but there again, I think the last time I stayed in a youth hostel was with Em and Gill at the grand old age of 16. It was our first holiday away with no parents and we opted for youth hostelling in Whitby, unlike some of today's 16 year olds who'd be partying hard in Ayia Napa, showing their arse and tits while they get shit-faced on tequila slammers.

In our youth, we thought that climbing up the drainpipe after curfew to squeeze unceremoniously through the toilet window in order to avoid the female Hermann Goering on guard at the reception desk, would be fun. We spent all our hard-earned pocket money on vodka instead of food and then avoided the ten o'clock lockdown by sleeping on an arse-crippling bench in the graveyard of Whitby Abbey. Yes! A GRAVEYARD! For some reason, this seemed like a reasonable thing to do, despite ending up with backsides that were colder than a polar bear's bollocks. With one eye open for the church warden, and the other on guard for the rising up of Whitby's living dead, a peaceful slumber was definitely not on the cards.

The youthful mind is a wonderfully stupid and naive thing, and looking back I'm seriously thankful that we got through those years without getting in harm's way. We were so determined to stay out past the ridiculously early deadline, that we even spent one night with some random lads we got chatting to in a pub. They were fortunately only after having a good time, and there was no funny business attempted. We just had an entertaining evening and a comfier bed than sleeping with Dracula's mates. It did turn out that they were known to the local police when we got stopped getting a ride in the back of their pickup truck… Ahhh the innocence of youth: where you believe you're completely invincible and the worst thing that can happen is you run out of vodka.

Despite the passing of the years, and confessions about many of my adventures during my youth, I still haven't come clean about our first unchaperoned jaunt to my Mum for fear that she may still get that look of disappointment that mothers are so good at. Sorry Mum.

Anyway, I had no intention of repeating any such shenanigans with my planned trip, no shimmying up drainpipes would be going on, not to mention squeezing though any windows with my now slightly curvier backside. Besides, I'm a mature sensible woman now… ha-ha.

I'd been sent the itinerary for the weekend, which was to start with drinks and a curry on the Friday evening, then a choice of guided walks on the Saturday followed by a barbeque (weather dependent – obviously, with it being the Lake District) and then another short walk before heading home on the Sunday. The little voice in my head kept telling me I could do this, but now it had come to actually going, I didn't want to go.

Unfortunately, the little confidence boosting voice had now been kicked into touch by the nagging doubtful one that kept pecking away whispering… 'You won't know anybody. They will all be boring gits or serial rapists. You'll be sleeping in a bunk bed with Bertha the Big Butt on top. Drinks will consist of a can of Barrs Shandy and you'll end up coming home early'.

Despite these little pessimistic murmurings, I'd paid the deposit and I'd be buggered if I was going to waste that. Besides I wasn't one to back away from a challenge, so locking my doubtful voice away, I decided to throw caution to the wind and go.

The weekend started in a bizarre fashion before I'd even got out of Manchester. I'd left work at a reasonable time, but due to an accident, the roads seemed to be more gridlocked than the M25 at nine o'clock on a weekday. For once I was happy to sit in traffic thinking that this may be the excuse I was looking for. Oh crap… Realisation hit that I'd inadvertently put my phone in the boot with the Bluetooth turned off and if I needed to call to make my apologies (thinking positively eh?) or ask for directions (likely), I would definitely be needing it. So, it was with the swiftness of a cornered carjacker that I jumped out of the car when we came to a standstill to retrieve it.

On seeing me rifling through the boot to locate

my elusive phone with more determination than a chav at a car boot sale, the bloke in the car behind shouted to me.

'Excuse me, but do you have a phone?' Nothing like asking the obvious eh, when I was stood there with a phone in my hand?

'Erm. Yes' was all I actually said, avoiding the temptation at sarcasm.

'I don't suppose you could call my wife could you? I've not got my phone, so if you could tell her I'm going to be late to take her to work so she'll need to walk that would be great.'

Oh good lord! …What could I say? 'NO' I can hear you screaming at the pages… 'You could have said 'NO' or just made up some lame excuse about not having credit,' but the poor bloke looked distraught, and I did have my phone in my hand, so I felt compelled to oblige.

He quickly put his number in just as the traffic started moving …bugger … I hastily jumped back in my car and dialled the number.

Me: 'Erm. Hello. You don't know me but your husband doesn't have his phone and is in the car behind. We're stuck in horrendous traffic so when he saw me getting my phone out of the boot he asked me to ring you to let you know he'll be late so you may need to start walking to work.'

Woman: 'Who are YOU?' said in an accusing tone.

Me: 'I'm in the car in front of your husband, and

as I was just getting my phone out of the boot, he asked me to ring you to say he'd be late as he doesn't have his phone on him' I'm sure I'd just explained all this.

Slightly mad woman: 'Well how do you know him and where's his phone?' said in an even more accusing tone.

Me: 'I don't know him, so I don't know where his phone is. He's just in the car behind and he saw I had a phone so asked if I could call to let you know.' *Was this woman hard of hearing or just mental?*

Annoyed woman: 'Well how long will he be?' said in an accusing and exasperated tone.

How the fuck should I know?

Me: 'I'm sorry I don't know because I don't know where you live.' *Bloody obvious.*

Irate woman: 'Put him on!!'

Me: 'I can't put him on because HE'S IN THE CAR BEHIND' *I'm sure I'd pointed this out several times already.*

Incensed woman: 'I want to speak to him NOW!' For the love of God, was this woman listening at all??

Me: 'HE IS IN THE CAR BEHIND. WE ARE IN TRAFFIC. I AM NOT GETTING OUT. HE JUST WANTED ME TO RING YOU SO THAT YOU WOULD KNOW HE WILL BE LATE!'

Christ, this woman was hardly The Brain of Britain, was she?

Stroppy bitch: 'Hmmph. Well I don't know how you REALLY know him, but don't you worry I'll be asking him when I see him, AND you can tell him from me, that I'm NOT happy and when I get back from work he better have a bloody good explanation.' Click.

OH ….MY…. GOD!!!

I was speechless as I just stared at the phone display on the dashboard in amazement. You try to do somebody a favour and that's what you get in return. Mind you, I actually felt sorrier for the poor sod she was married to. Had we not started to move at pace I would have got out of the car and told him to divorce the mentally unstable lunatic.

Having no doubt broken up a marriage by trying to be a Good Samaritan, I continued on my journey pondering the possibilities of having to change my number to avoid the wrath of the unhinged nut job who now thought I was somehow involved with her poor abused husband.

The only benefit of this little incident, was that it had briefly taken my mind off the up-and-coming weekend for a bit, but as I left the motorway the niggling doubts once again invaded my thoughts and I started to feel more apprehensive than a contestant on *X Factor* who can't sing and doesn't have a dead relative story to trot out.

So that I didn't get horrendously lost, I'd programmed the postcode of the hostel into my Sat Nav, or Aida as I like to call her; this is for no other reason than it conjures up the image of a helpful old lady aiding my journey …get it? I know… it's tenuous at best, but I've stuck with it. Although Aida had always successfully navigated many a journey, she does have a habit of taking me on the most bizarre route sometimes, maybe the quickest way as the crow flies, but as I don't have feathers or wings, I've ended up down lanes that you'd struggle getting a fat bloke on a pushbike down not to mention an Audi A1. This seemed to be the case too on this little jaunt, as I set off down a narrow lane…for nine miles.

By the time I'd got half way I was beginning to think Aida had finally lost her mind, not to mention me. Thank God it was light still, or I'd have felt like Alice on her way to Wonderland passing through a rabbit hole as the hedges closed in around me. Where in God's name was the daft old bint taking me?

Having not seen any signs of civilisation for some time I was beginning to contemplate that this was in fact the Road to Nowhere that Talking Heads had been on, and I'd be stuck driving round until I finally ran out of petrol or patience depending which came first. After not hearing a peep out of my automated driving companion for what seemed like hours, Aida suddenly woke up from what must have been her evening doze to finally pipe up, 'You have reached your destination'.

'Where? Where the hell is my destination you crazy woman?' Yes, I was a little bit crabby and stressed with her at this point as I unglued my fingers from the steering wheel and looked around for a building. Just a few yards ahead I could see some trees and what looked like an entrance. Oh Crap! I really was staying in the middle of nowhere. I pulled into the drive and abandoned my car alongside the other vehicles that looked like they'd been randomly strewn across the area at the front of the house. Well this was it. I was here. No turning back now... I felt sick!

To be fair the hostel looked quite nice from the outside, and it was in a lovely setting even if it was just a little too remote for my liking. This was certainly getting away from it all, I'd be lucky if they had electricity and running water never mind a phone signal.

Once inside, the décor could be best described as rustic with threadbare carpets that had obviously seen many a walking boot trampling the pile to within a millimetre of the floorboards, and yellow paintwork that could be matched to the gnashers of a 50-a-day chain smoking coffee addict. I think that the paint companies are missing a trick there with a new shade of nicotine white.

The shabby not so chic hallway had two rooms either side, a set of stairs leading up to the next floor and then another corridor at the far end leading to God knows where. As there seemed to be nobody about I peered tentatively into the first room on the right; this turned out to be a large lounge area with a mismatch of sofas that looked like they'd been sourced from a number of skips in the dead of night. The room however was empty. Christ where was everybody?

The second area was the dining room, well when

I say dining room this makes it sound a little more ornate than it actually was. It essentially consisted of about ten long tables that were covered with plastic tablecloths with benches either side to park your backside on. You could have been forgiven for thinking you'd stumbled upon a remote trucker's café where the only things missing were the bottles of ketchup and smell of stale chip fat. At the far end, there was also a serving hatch into the kitchen and, halle-bloody-lujah, some people! As I nervously approached the hatch, the bloke behind the counter spotted me.

'Hi. You must be Isobel, I'm Matt'. He had a warm friendly face and a welcoming manner and, as he knew my name, I was guessing he was the organiser or the group psychic.

'Hi. Yes, although Izzy's fine as only my mother calls me Isobel and then only when I'm in trouble,' I was going for a bit of humour from the get-go. 'I've just parked my car at the front, is that okay?'

'Yeah that's fine, although if you make sure you're parked in close to the other cars as we have to block each other in so all the cars fit.'

What? Blocked in? Gulp…. That means even if I want to escape I can't. This was the first thought that raced into my panicked little brain, although in reality, as the drive here had been a tad harrowing, and the place was more difficult to find than Big Foot's mountain retreat, the likelihood of me driving back tonight in the dark was on a par with winning the lottery.

'Okay, thanks. I'll just go and move up a bit and get my stuff out then.'

When I returned carrying my holdall and supply of wine, Matt was waiting with a much-needed glass of Pimms, Hmmm.... Maybe this was going to be an okay weekend after all. He introduced me to an equally friendly lady called Pam, who I was told I'd be sharing the dorm with.

Pam kindly offered to take me up to the room and give me the guided tour. This consisted of showing me the lounge, looking just as random and empty as it had before, pointing out the toilets and shower rooms and then taking us to our dormitory where there were two sets of bunk beds and a wardrobe that I think had been retrieved from the same skip as the sofas judging by the knocks and scrapes it had.

She reliably informed me that we'd be sharing with one other lady, who'd already put dibs on one of the bottom bunks and, as she had laid claim to the remaining lower one, I had the unenviable task of choosing between the two top ones. Great. The last time I'd slept on the top bunk was when I was about ten, and half the size I am now.

Next came the challenge of making the bed. Part of the joys of lodging in a youth hostel is that you have to do everything for yourself including fighting with a plastic mattress that was about as flexible as a brick whilst balancing on a set of wooden ladders designed for a five-year-old.

Having been left alone to complete this arduous challenge, I fucked and double fucked abusively as the sheet that was designed for a cot wouldn't stretch from one corner to the other without making the mattress look like a curled-up piece of cod…. And as for the quilt… I've seen tramps begging down Market Street sat on thicker duvets. It's a good job they'd supplied us with a blanket made out of horse hair and Brillo pads to compensate!

So, after my epic tussle with the bedding, and numerous unsuccessful attempts to send messages to friends asking them to never let me book anything again whilst in an inebriated state, I finally ventured downstairs to meet the rest of the walking group.

It seemed, as I entered the hub of activity in the kitchen, that I was the only person who didn't know somebody or hadn't been on one of these events before. To say I felt like a fish out of water as I stood very self-consciously sipping my drink is like saying that *Jaws* felt a little out of place riding a bike.

The first person to come and introduce himself was a bloke who looked to be in his early fifties called John. Let's just analyse his introduction, shall we?

'Hi I'm John. Is this your first weekend as I've not seen you before?' *Non-offensive and polite.*

Having introduced myself back and confirmed that yes it was indeed my first weekend, this was his follow up statement….

'The first time I came on one of these weekends

my father died.' *Dear God... What the hell do you say to that?*

'Oh, I'm sorry.' Was just about all I could think of. It turned out that while he'd been inaugurating himself into the world of walking weekends, his father had sadly passed away from a heart attack, so not a horrendous walking accident as a result of negligence then! He went on to tell me how he now lived with his Mother (hmmm I can't say I was surprised) but was determined to still come on the weekends as a dedication to his Dad who'd loved walking too. This led to numerous mind-numbing tales about all the walks they'd been on together, all of which were about as riveting as a lecture on crop rotation.

My eyes were just beginning to glaze over from sheer boredom, and I was contemplating if his Dad wasn't in fact dead, but had just taken the opportunity to abscond and was now living happily in Thailand with his new 20 year old bride, when I was rescued in the nick of time by what I can only describe as a scouse double act called Billy and Bobby.

They were certainly a breath of fresh air after the dull reminiscing from John; it'd be like comparing a luxury facial to root canal treatment. Billy was the chattier of the two, although Bobby was equally as funny when he could get a word in. They'd been on lots of these weekends together but had known each other since school so had many a tale to tell of their escapades together, most of which involved drink, women and worryingly, hospital visits.

As the wine flowed we moved to the dining area to eat our curry. I'm not sure that under the Trade Descriptions Act 'curry' is a term that would hold up in court for the practically luminous yellow-looking stew that was served up, but it tasted okay and came with rice and poppadoms.

Having paid a visit earlier to the loos, I was a bit worried about the effects that the toxic concoction would have on my guts, so I chose to pick at the glowing bits of chicken and just eat the rice to be on the safe side.

We were joined on our table by Pam and another lady called Susan who it turned out was my fellow roommate. Despite my anxieties, I actually had a really pleasant evening with lots of laughter as they gave me the lowdown on a few of the more colourful characters in the group.

There was a couple at the far end of the room who apparently were into S&M. Yes, I have got that the right way around and I'm not going to tell you about couple who only shopped at M&S. Hell No… this pair were both into sadomasochism big time, and freely admitted this after a large number of wines at one of these events. I know I'm generalising when I say they didn't look the type. She was sat there in her Berghaus, no make-up and hair that resembled my blanket, and he would have looked more at home at a train station with a notebook and pen, so I couldn't see them exchanging the wool and fleece for rubber and chains if I'm honest. They had even confessed to having hooks in their bedroom ceiling and a collection of whips that Cynthia Payne would be proud of. I know what you're thinking. That they were winding me up as I am after all, a gullible idiot, but they assured me that it was true, and surely they wouldn't make something like that up about somebody. Would they?

Then there was Phileas Fogg Horn… who didn't really need an introduction, as my ears thought that we'd been moved to a blast zone when he arrived slightly later than everybody else and boomed 'HELLO EVERYBODY!!' at a level that made Brian Blessed seem like a timid little mouse. I swear that birds within a ten-mile radius dropped out of the trees and then packed up their little nests to move to a safe distance, perhaps Outer Mongolia, as he continued to talk and laugh at the same volume throughout the evening recounting tales of his travels. It seemed like he'd been everywhere, no doubt leaving a trail of devastation and deaf people behind.

Fortunately, after the dinner, he moved to the lounge area, so with all the doors shut it reduced the volume to mere normal conversation level. I could tell the poor bastards he'd been sat next to as they made their escape to bed early complaining of ringing in their ears. The fear being that, were they to spend another minute with him, this could easily turn into the more permanent tinnitus, hence spurring on their departure. He should have come with a health warning and a pair of ear defenders for anybody he talked to. God, I prayed he wasn't on my walk tomorrow.

There was also a walrus of a woman, taking up

half a bench at the table in the corner, who looked like a cross between a Russian shot putter and Shergar. Combining her huge teeth, that matched the paintwork, with biceps that were so big she looked like she could snap you in half with her little finger and throw both pieces of you to the other side of the Lake District without breaking out into so much as a sweat. I hoped that she wasn't on a top bunk or the poor sod below would spend a very restless night waiting to have the life crushed out of them if the bunk had not been weight tested by a tree trunk. She looked about as much like a walker as Ozzy Osbourne. Had they told me she was into S&M I could well have believed it, although I'm sure she'd be the one doing the whipping; it would take a very brave man with balls of steel to even *think* about inflicting pain on this woman. Unbelievably though, she apparently was a bit of a man-eater. This was probably through intimidation rather than sex appeal, although many of her relationships had ended with restraining orders and probably a beloved pet boiling on the stove. Nearly every eligible male in the group had been on the receiving end of her carnal desires and several had even succumbed…. including Billy!

'What on God's earth made you do that….and more importantly how the hell did you live to tell the tale?' was my question to him once I'd stopped laughing.

'I'd had a shit load of wine and I'd not had a shag for over a year!' was the poor excuse given.

That's men for you. Better to have sex with a

rampant bull of a woman than go home to an empty house for a meal for one and an evening of masturbation. However, he'd at least managed to escape a repeat of the shenanigans and the re-homing of his pet, as throughout their romp, despite his best efforts - or so he said - he had failed to satisfy her. His actual phrase was that 'it was like putting his todger into the Mersey tunnel and expecting it to touch the sides'. She, on the other hand, had given him a unique blow job, that he compared to putting his penis in the end of a Dyson whilst listening to Tiddles coughing up a fur ball. Yuck! I'm still not sure I believed all of the tall tales I was told, but it did make for a very entertaining evening and given my initial apprehension, a very enjoyable one.

We eventually retired to our dorms at about half past one in the morning having consumed the best part of the weekend's supply of wine in one night. I hadn't even considered the fact that I would need to climb up to the top bunk but, as it turns out, copious amounts of alcohol inhibited any fears of falling out of a narrow wooden cot, until, that is, I woke up the next day and had to climb down swaying more than a dingy in the Atlantic Ocean.

It was now time to brave the bathroom facilities, as I quietly grabbed my toiletries to go for an early morning shower in the hope of clearing my head....

Although there were male and female amenities in the hostel, they were neither clearly marked nor that private with open doorways to each. As you stood at said doorways, you could clearly see the two large sinks opposite; these looked more apt for washing pots than people with a capacity for at least five dinner services and a small child. You then only had to move in slightly to be able to see the two small toilet cubicles that had neither functioning locks nor full doors; not great for any morning ablutions! Then there were the two shower stalls. These were located on the left-hand side, thankfully out of plain sight from the doorway, however they were only partially obscured by what can only be described as a piece of cling film.

If there was a competition for how quick you could actually have a shower, I think I'd be in with a good chance of winning as I dived in, washed, unstuck the shower curtain from my backside, rinsed, unstuck the shower curtain from my backside *again* and got out in about one minute flat. These wonderful bathroom facilities meant that by the end of the weekend my hair would look like the contents of a chip pan and my poo would be backed up more than the M60 in rush hour. There was no way I was staying in there long enough to wash my hair, and having anything other than a wee was most definitely out of the question.

After my nanosecond shower, I went down for breakfast and to help make the mountain of butties that were being supplied for the walk. This involved spreading I Can Believe it's not Butter - because it tastes like oil - onto doughy value bread and topping with slimy ham that had less pig in it than a Jewish butcher's shop…Hmm I was looking forward to them.

The weather fortunately, was gorgeous, as we set off in convoy for the less strenuous walk around Buttermere. The walk was stunning showing off all the best qualities that the beautiful Lake District is famous for: the awe-inspiring mountain ranges, the sparkling lakes, the fresh country air, the little tea shops selling homemade cakes and creamy Lakeland Ice Cream, and …bugger me, NO peace and quiet!

All the way around Phileas Frigging Fogg Horn went on and on and on about every topic under the sun from, how he once owned his own funeral director's business, he probably had a few corpses come back from the dead to tell him to, 'Shut the fuck up. Let us rest in peace', to how he was looking for a woman to share his life and travels with now he was retired. I suggested he look on Match.com for a deaf mute as the poor cow would never get a word in and not being able to hear him rabbiting on like a broken record at a volume to rival The Big Bang is the only way that any woman could put up with him.

By the time we got back to the hostel, I'd really had enough of the small talk and the loud talk and would have liked nothing better than to drive home with my ringing ears to the sanctuary of my little house, but as I would have needed the driving abilities of Evil Knievel to get my car out, I was stuck for the final night. The promised barbeque turned out to be pie and mash, but after the late night on the Friday, the long walk today with motor-mouth, and a few wines, I was really flagging to remain sociable. So, once the food was cleared away, I took the earliest opportunity to make my excuses and retired to my bunk bed to rest my devastated ear drums.

The following morning saw us all mucking in to clear up the hostel before our departure. All beds had to be unmade, the kitchen had to be cleaned, and all the empties from the Friday and Saturday nights drinking thrown into a *very* large bin. Given my history with bins I avoided this task.

Another walk was planned for that day but, safe in the knowledge that if I spent another few hours in the company of the human megaphone I would probably have to spend the next 20 years being somebody's bitch in prison, I told a little white lie saying that I was going to visit a friend in the Lakes on the way back, so I'd have to miss the walk.

All in all, it hadn't been an awful weekend; some bits I'd really enjoyed. I'd also met some really nice people, but on reflection booking a weekend away with a bunch of strangers is something that had been so far out of my comfort zone it would be like Pavarotti putting his name down for the Triathlon.

I'm glad I did it though; it's always good to try new things but I don't think that I'll be booking another one any time soon…certainly not until I've either lost my hearing or think Bondage in the Brecon Beacons is on my bucket list.

20

The Key to a Good Relationship...

Contrast this experience with a weekend away with Peter a few weeks later, and they could not be further apart. I'm not talking distance in miles, as we'd opted for a little shaggathon in the Lake District. What better place to hide away for a weekend of exhilarating walks followed by fantastic beer, gorgeous locally-sourced food and some damn good sex?

We'd booked a little cottage not far from Bowness-On-Windermere so we had everything on our doorstep; I was also familiar with the good places to take Ferdinand. Peter had only been to the Lakes once and that was many years before, so it was all relatively new to him. It was fantastic to bore the pants off him as I did my best impression of Alfred Wainwright pointing out what I called Three Bumps Pike and Huge Hillock. Okay I admit it, after years of going to the Lake District I could no more work out which mountain was which than knit a sock out of cloud.

Things were going really well; the cottage was

beautiful and I hadn't had this much fun for quite some time. Peter was great company and we were getting on like a house on fire. What a bizarre phrase that is…why would turning somebody's residence to ash and cinder be a good thing? Getting on like chocolate and orange, now that would be better as it's an immense combination. Maybe even, getting on like Bonnie and Clyde…oh hang on though, didn't they end up dead? Well, whatever the phrase, we were having a fantastic time together. For a change, the one absolute cock-up of the holiday was surprisingly not down to me.

After a long walk on the Saturday, that had completely exhausted Ferdinand to the point that he was now curled up snoozing, delightfully dreaming about chomping on the bone *little* Cedric had been getting his teeth into, we decided to take a chance and leave him to drive down to Bowness for a quick drink and pick up a takeaway. We wouldn't be gone long and it would take something on the scale of Mount Vesuvius erupting to wake the pooch from his dog-tired slumber.

We had a couple of relaxing drinks while the curry was being prepared. It was only when we got back to the cottage with the deliciously smelling spicy delights that Peter went to get the key and the trauma unfolded.

'Fucking hell. I can't find the key!'

'Ha-ha. Stop kidding. Come on the curry will be getting cold and I'm sure you can't wait to get your hands on my bhajis not to mention me getting my mouth around your shish kebab'. Yes, I know, *Carry on*

Curry night was in full swing.

'I'm not kidding. It was in my pocket one minute, and now it's gone' Houdini eat your heart out.

Now, I don't know if you've rented a cottage recently, but the new thing seems to be that, instead of collecting the key from some spotty, grumpy bored teenager working Saturdays at the local rental offices, you now have a key safe on the outside that you're given the code to prior to arrival. What you are also advised to do is lock the keys back in there when you go out, so as not to lose them. It's a damn shame I didn't remind Peter of this before we went out for the evening!

'Let's just look in the car to see if it's dropped out. I'm sure it'll be here somewhere.' The voice of calm and experience here.

It was then like watching an episode of *Scrapheap Challenge* as we practically dismantled the car in the futile search for the elusive key. When the final piece of the car had been pulled to bits, Peter progressed from being mildly agitated to total hair-pulling anxiety, as he began to panic more than Dracula stuck in a tanning booth.

'Fuck! Where can it be? Oh my God! Ferdinand's in the cottage, what are we going to do?'

Bloody hell, I never saw myself as the level-headed one, but as Peter paced back and forth like a caged tiger on speed, I took control in an effort to calm him down.

'It's okay. We'll just re-trace our steps and go back to the pubs and the curry house to see if anybody has handed it in.' Logical suggestion.

So after having checked the surrounding area and the interior of the car for the millionth time, just in case the keys had been in an alternate universe for the last hour, we drove back down to Bowness with my car smelling like Madhur Jaffrey's kitchen. I decided to save time by waiting in the car outside each place while Peter popped in to see if the key had been handed in. I could tell as his shoulders slouched lower and lower down to the ground with each successive place that his search was in vain. Each time he approached the car his face dropped and he was wringing his hands in agitation more and more, by the time he came out of the curry house he looked like the animated offspring of Droopy and Monty Burns.

'Fuck! Fuck! Fuck! What are we going to do? It's Saturday night so there'll be nobody in the office. Fuck! And Ferdinand is in there. FUCK! What an idiot. I've never lost a key in my life. I'm so careful all the time, I don't know what happened. Where could it be? Oh my God! We are going to have to break in to get him out! Did you leave a window open? We could perhaps climb through if we have… well you could as I don't think I'd fit... Oh shit! I am soooo sorry'.

I had visions of having to slap him or at the very least get a bag for him to breathe into to calm him down.

'It's okay. I've got the number of the owner so I'll give her a call to see if there's a spare key we can pick up.' Good lord it was a good job one of us had the ability to think in a crisis, who'd have thought that would be me?

Mind you I have had a few experiences of losing keys over the years... To be fair though, on one of these occasions I didn't actually lose it as such, but it was more unobtainable as my ex had driven off with my handbag in the car having dropped me off at home. Being the excellent planner that he is, and knowing what I'm like, he'd put a spare somewhere.... Now if only I had paid better attention as to where. Don't be fooled into thinking that he'd just put the key somewhere safe that I could easily find though. Oh no. He had made this a challenge fit for Ethan Hunt.

It was a particularly shitty and rainy day as I recall - well, a summer's day in Manchester - so there I was in my high heels wading across our extremely muddy lawn to find the first key.... Yes! First!

Having scrambled in the bushes to get to the garden ornament where *numero uno* key was stealthily hidden, I made my way back across the mud pit trying not to slip unceremoniously onto my backside. Have you ever seen stilettos turned into wedges by mud? I don't think that Dolce & Gabbana will be adding it to their winter collection; I'm not sure about Vivien Westwood though. Still, at least I could now open the garage to give me access to the second key.

Now, where in God's name did he say it was? Although we were one of those rare breeds that actually put their car in the garage and didn't just use it as a dumping ground, it still had quite a lot of junk in it: multiple old paint tins, where the white now looked like you'd squeezed a particularly big spot into the tin, old walking boots that leaked and smelt worse than week-old broccoli and stilton soup, I even had a bike in there, and the last time I'd rode it I'd had to have my hands prized from the handle bars because I'd been gripping on tighter than Jeremy Corbyn onto the Labour leadership.

So, with feet clogged in mud and clothes that looked like I'd been water cannoned, the hunt was on to find the hidden *numero dos* key. It took me 30 minutes of grumbling, cursing and shivering to complete this task, but eventually I found the key in a bucket on a shelf high enough that even in heels was only just in reaching distance. I ask you, who puts a key in a bucket on a top shelf when you are a family that are short enough to make *The Borrowers* seem tall?

Anyway, this now gave me access to the cubby hole where *el numero tres* and final key was. The only problem was that this cupboard was also known as The Creepy Crawly Cupboard, as it seemed that my Australian adversary, Boris, had legions of British relations who had built a housing estate in there.

As you may have guessed though, my overly cautious husband had concealed this right at the back. I was now in an episode of *I'm a Celebrity Get me Out of Here*, although I'm ever so slightly less famous than the has-beens and reality totty that they have on there.

I gingerly leaned in trying to avoid the humungous cobweb that would capture a small pony never mind a fly. If that was the cobweb I'd hate to see the size of the bugger that made it. Oh, and there he was; Boris's Pommy cousin guarding the key with a ferocity matched only by a bull terrier with anger management issues. Still, nothing that a sharp stick couldn't move. You didn't think I was going to put my hand in, did you?

I eventually got in the house having completed my challenge, looking like I'd just emerged from an underground tomb. All this effort had meant that I'd got in the house a whole *five* minutes before my husband got back!

Anyway, back to the evolving drama in the Lakes where I hoped the proprietor of the cottage would not be a fan of *The Crystal Maze* with a desire to put any stupidly clumsy holidaymaker through such an audaciously planned key retrieval process. So, it was with trepidation and a few prayers that they were not out partying the night away, that I phoned the owner. It rang out for what seemed like a lifetime, while Peter sat next to me still doing his Droopy Burns impression.

'Hello' *Thank you God*!!!

'Hi. I'm really sorry to disturb you, but we're renting Swallow Croft Cottage and (*the imbecile sat next to me*) we seem to have lost the key. I don't suppose you have a spare that we could come and pick up, do you? I am really sorry.'

'Oh …I don't live locally I'm afraid, but we do

have one spare just in case. We keep it in a safe box at the back of the cottage.' I could visibly see the relief flood into Peter as he mouthed the words, 'Thank fuck for that!' It seemed spontaneous profanities were a side effect of stress for Peter.

She gave us the code and details of where to find the box; no scaling onto the roof or digging up a map with our bare hands, thank goodness. She did stress though that it was the *only* spare so could we please make sure we didn't lose this one. I didn't think Peter would be making that mistake again, in fact he'd already abdicated as the key holder and renounced all responsibility for the rest of the weekend. Hallelujah!

We drove back to the cottage in a slightly less fraught state. Well I did. Peter was still jiggling about like he'd got a bunch of stinging nettles up his arse; he wouldn't be happy until he'd got the key and was in the cottage. He flew out the car quicker than a greyhound on acid, but having only heard the words, 'at the back of the cottage', he darted to the right and began to clamber behind the row of cottages to get to ours which was located at the end… on the left! Why in God's name he thought that you would need to negotiate your way all along the brambled bank at the rear of all the cottages to get to the back of ours was beyond me, but it seemed that common sense was not as forthcoming as swearing. It did make an entertaining sight though, when he got there to find me with the key already out of the safe.

Ferdinand, of course, was oblivious to nearly being abandoned and left to fend for himself, as he slept soundly on his nice comfy bed in the lovely warm cottage. Let's face it though, there would hardly have been the need to get Paul O'Grady involved on the grounds of animal cruelty as a result of him being left for the night. My fate on the other hand, would have been to spend the night in A&E after having to squeeze my back side through a window that an anorexic dwarf would have struggled to get through.

21

Home Invasion of the Creepy Kind

My life had now settled down into a nice routine of work, sex, walking Ferdinand, drinking and more sex. After months of not knowing if I was coming or going I was finally beginning to think that life was good and the orgasms were even better. That was until a couple of squirrels came into my world; yes, you did read that correctly...squirrels!

It all started when a couple of the fury blighters, I named Freddy and Freda, decided to take up residence in my loft. For a few weeks, I could hear them scurrying and scratching in the night as they did the squirrel fandango in hobnail boots into the wee small hours. I'd almost been at the point of ringing the landlord to see if he wanted to go up there to check...there was no way I was sticking my head up into the loft space to get my face ripped off by a rabid and angry couple of fluffy vermin. Peter also declined my kind offer to let him go and check too. Wuss!

I'd stayed at Peter's for the weekend so returned

home a tad exhausted but with a smile on my face that was so fixed that it would've given Brian Cox a run for his money. As an aside, is that man ever miserable? Every time you see him on TV he's grinning like a ventriloquist dummy, and similarly, it never changes the whole time he's talking. I think he's got a switch at the back of his head that's stuck on GRIN. I'm not criticising him though, it's way better to have a smile on your face, but really, does it have to be all the time? I've seen more movement in the face of an overly plasticised movie star. The world probably needs more Brian Cox's though, but maybe not if you have certain roles in society; if you're a newsreader or a funeral director for instance. Grinning like an idiot while you deliver a sombre piece of news about the latest crisis in the Middle East could spark some sort of international incident. Equally, a happy smiling face beaming at you after you've just viewed your poor deceased relative, could be a tad insensitive.

Anyway, having quickly unpacked my little overnight bag and jumped in the shower to revive my tired limbs, I returned to the bedroom and noticed what looked like a grain of rice on the windowsill. I'd had the windows open the previous day so thought nothing of it as I disposed of it down the toilet. As I returned to the bedroom to dry my hair, I noticed another grain of rice. Odd, but again, thought little of it. Then I moved the washing basket… Holy Crap!!

Underneath it was a large cluster of pale and

disgusting maggots all squirming around in an effort to hide after having been cruelly exposed. I let out a little squeal and jumped back like a scalded cat. I then began to inspect the rest of the bedroom ……and wished I hadn't. There were maggots hiding absolutely everywhere. In fact, the unscrupulous little bastards seemed to have the ability to find every dark little crevice they could wriggle their squirmy bodies into.

I moved around the room like a cussing ninja, gently lifting bits of furniture to look underneath. 'What the heck?', 'Bloody Nora', 'Holy Shit', and then the big crescendo as I leaned down to look under my bed 'Fucking Hell.'

Thankfully, Ferdinand was still at my Mum and Dad's or my main concern would have been to make sure he didn't think they were a nice tasty nutritious snack; as we know he'll eat anything so would've thought nothing of tucking into a nice maggot or two.

Before I could tackle the problem of where they were coming from though, I first had to get rid of the ones that were currently using my bedroom as a maggot knocking shop to breed quicker than a catholic prostitute on IVF. How the hell do you get rid of maggots? There was definitely far too many to pick up and put down the toilet; the amount of toilet paper required would exceed any teenage boy's weekly quota, not to mention the blockage a ton of maggots and loo roll would cause. Sweeping them up was maybe an option, but as I only possessed a hand brush and pan, I decided that getting on my hands and knees in a scene that resembled *Night of the Living Dead* was best to be avoided. There was only one thing for it…the hoover. Although this would result in me having to buy a new one, at least I could avoid direct contact, so long as I didn't fall in the bin after them!

Oh. My. God. It was disgusting, and something that will be etched in my brain for eternity, as I watched the maggot tornado swirl around the cylinder as the hoover got fuller and fuller.

I moved every bit of furniture, getting in all the corners to make sure that I'd got every last one of the little bastards, before having to think about emptying the hoover. I was like a woman possessed as I then cleaned all the skirting boards with a tough cleaning agent, following up with a liberal dose of antibacterial spray. I wasn't sure what germs they carried, but I was taking no chances in fumigating the bedroom to the standard of *Obsessive Compulsive Cleaners* with a fetish for the smell of bleach. Convinced that nothing could have survived this maggot holocaust, I began to put everything back before facing the task of getting rid of the hoover.

Oh my fucking giddy aunt!!!

As I put the washing basket back I couldn't believe what I was seeing, more had appeared with skills only seen at the annual conference of the Magic Circle. Was it the washing basket they were coming from? I quickly took it outside and hoovered the offending pupae up before they could escape into the recesses of the bedroom. All thoughts that I'd finally found the source of the maggot eruption was however short lived, as I turned around to face the window only to be greeted with the sight of more of the little buggers on the windowsill and the carpet below. I wanted to cry, all my hard work and cleaning had been in vain. This was getting beyond horrific and the hoover was getting beyond full. Time to ring the landlord. In all his 25 years of renting properties I'm sure he had never had a phone call quite like it.

'Hi, it's Isobel Parkes here. I'm sorry to trouble you on a Sunday, but I need you to come around please. I have maggots appearing out of thin air all over my bedroom carpet and I don't know what to do.'

I'm sure he must have thought I was on drugs, drunk, totally insane or all three. To his credit though, he came around pretty sharpish, probably more to check that his tenant wasn't tripping on LSD than to check the invasion of the maggots.

Having seen that I wasn't on some mad hallucinogenic narcotics, and that there were indeed maggots on the bedroom carpet, he quickly disappeared to get his steam cleaner. He was convinced that boiling the buggers while they hid in the carpet waiting to explode into action would solve the problem, and to be fair it did…for a while.

We pulled the carpet away from the skirting boards to reveal any crafty blighters that were lurking underneath waiting until all the commotion was over.

This was followed by a generous sprinkling of anti-pest powder in an effort to kill any that may emerge at a later date.

I'd left Ferdinand at my Mum's explaining that I'd been infested with maggots. This caused a reaction that was similar to telling her that I had some fatal disease; immediately offering to send my Dad round to help and insisting that I move back home at once. Having calmed her down and reassured her that I was not about to be devoured by maggots while I slept, I settled down to a very very …let's add another one in capitals for effect…. VERY restless night.

I know what you're thinking. You think that I'm absolutely stark-raving bonkers to have stayed in the bedroom whilst there was still a prospect that there could be more maggots lurking to eat my flesh in the night. As I felt that the steam-cleaning had obliterated every last one though, I wanted to stick it out in a foolish act of stubborn bravery. Besides, I didn't want to leave the house and come back from work the following day to find the carpet had once again taken on a life of its own. The only hope was to pray that boiling, bleaching and fumigating them had worked. I did manage to nod off slightly whilst listening to the soothing tinkle of the rain on the window.

In the morning when I turned the lamp on, it became clear that I'd not in fact been lulled to sleep by the gentle sound of the precipitation falling outside, but the 'tink' 'tink' of maggots dropping INSIDE!

Hold onto your hats though, as this is where it gets worse......

The maggots had been dropping all night from the ceiling, mainly by the window but also from the light fitting; above my bed!! I jumped out of bed quicker than a frog with a coiled spring loaded up his little amphibious backside. What I didn't consider, however, was what was on the carpet as I got out. Yuk!! Despite the fact that I'd squashed some of the buggers on my way out, this did not make me feel any better as I peeled them off the bottom of my bare feet. I then literally scraped half the skin off giving myself the most brutal pedicure imaginable.

After showering under steaming hot water, in a vain attempt to cleanse my body and mind from the gross experience I'd just endured, I limped to the kitchen and make a brew to kick start my brain enough to formulate a plan. This however, did not last long as the stress returned with a vengeance at the sight of yet more maggots downstairs!

I'll not write down the whole tirade of abusive language that escaped my lips, but needless to say, Sweary Mary would have blushed with embarrassment. I also must confess that at this point that I did blub like a baby. It didn't solve anything but by God I needed it.

I obviously couldn't go to work, so I rang and spoke to my manager, it's certainly the most bizarre excuse to take a Monday off I think she'll ever hear.

'Hi. I'm sorry but I need to take today off if that's

okay? My house looks like a horror movie set, with maggots all over the floor as they drop from the ceiling. And, I've scrubbed my feet so much I look like I've had a pedicure from Genghis Khan.' Who could say no to that?

My next call was to the landlord.

'Morning. It's Isobel again. You know how we thought the maggots were in the carpet? Well it turns out they're dropping from the ceiling so I think we may need pest control to sort it.'

My revelation that it had been raining maggots, and not men as The Weather Girls had so gleefully promised us, was met with irritating scepticism as he said that they couldn't possibly be dropping from the ceiling. *'They sodding are, and onto my bed too!' I wanted to shout.*

'Well could you sort it please as they're coming from somewhere and, sharing my house and my bed with a load of undeveloped larvae is a part of the tenancy agreement I don't recall signing up for.' Maybe a tad sarcastic but understandable as I was *very* stressed.

He gave me the number of a pest controller he'd used before who would hopefully be able to come out today. Hopefully?? He better had, or I'd be a gibbering swearing wreck and he'd be looking for a new tenant. Fortunately, the pest control man was really nice; I think the crying, panic and unashamed begging probably helped, but he agreed to come out as soon as he could. Phew!

I wanted to show him the house of horrors in its full ghastly glory so I left the maggots where they were, but hemmed them in with a barricade of the powder that made the Great Wall of China look like a small garden enclosure. The powder was enough to keep the most determined of invaders in their place. If by some miracle, one managed to burrow its way to freedom, they would then be met on the other side by a stern-faced mad woman with an Electrolux and a mission to suck up any absconders into oblivion.

The pest man, who turned out to be called Lionel, arrived about an hour later. I don't know why, but it just doesn't seem a very apt name for a pest man. You know how certain names conjure up images of certain jobs? Well to me, Lionel is an arty name, so would be more suited to directing a West End musical or making your hair look like something out of a hairspray commercial with just a pair of scissors and a set of curling tongs. Instead, this Lionel turned up looking like an extra on *Silent Witness* and carrying a pair of ladders and a loft probe. Mind you he could have been called Fred West and I would have let him in to look at my cavity walls if it got rid of the maggots.

After having shown him the apprehended maggots in the various locations across the house, he immediately identified them as fly larvae. Inevitably though, this meant that there was a dead body located in the vicinity. I don't think he was insinuating that I'd stowed away a rotting corpse in the confines of the airing cupboard, but more likely that some sort of vermin had inconsiderately passed away and was now fly food in the confines of the property. As the maggots were dropping, not like flies but like fly larvae, predominantly from the ceiling in the bedroom, his first port of call was the loft area.

I now had images of the Lionel dancing on my ceiling as he climbed up the ladder, however, this Lionel was looking more like a man about to enter a room of infectious diseases than a pop legend. As he lifted the door I stood well back for fear that thousands of maggots would drop from above. It didn't take him long to locate the source of the infestation: two dead squirrels!!

It seemed Freddy and Freda had danced their last fandango. Their poor rotting carcasses had become the breeding ground for thousands of maggots, who were now inhabiting my loft space. I can only imagine what it looked like up there… scratch that…. I *don't want* to imagine what it looked like up there.

Having bagged up and removed the dead dancing squirrels, he then sprayed the whole area with insecticide. Unfortunately, this would not spell the end of the daily maggot shower. It seemed that the intrepid bastards had already wriggled their germy little way into the cavity walls and any other nooks and crannies, and would have to work their way out to drop into the house.

As the days progressed, fewer appeared although it did become a bit of an obsession coming home each night to count the maggots. Maybe ITV should start a show where the contestant has to endure nights of bottom clenching terror, wondering what is going to drop on them in the night!

But don't think that this was the end of this HORRIFIC tale... What do maggots turn in to? Big horrible buzzing germ-spreading flies!

Instead of the house being infused with the beautiful aroma of fresh linen potpourri, it now reeked of bleached dead flies. My comfortable little house no longer felt like a safe haven that I could come home to and relax in. This was the *House of Horrors* that would forever feel infested, dirty and germ ridden. I would also never be able to eat egg fried rice again!

There was nothing for it. It was time to move.

22

Through the Keyhole

Before deciding where I wanted to move, I first had to think about, did I want to rent again or take the plunge and buy somewhere? As the mantra of 'You Must Own Your Own Home' had been instilled in me since I got my first tooth, I decided that for the same price as renting I could get a mortgage until I was 80. This would mean that eventually I'd own my own home, but unfortunately by then, probably not my own teeth.

And so began the hunt for the perfect place to see me into my ripe old age. I did think about moving directly into sheltered accommodation for the elderly. It seems, however, that rules exist to prevent you doing this. Apparently, you need to be deemed old enough to require the services of Reginald, the onsite warden who's on constant standby for a rapid response in the event you pull the red emergency cord that lights up his control panel like a Harrods Christmas tree.

As this wasn't an option though, I set about the task of finding somewhere I wanted to live; not easy when you have a monthly budget that is less than Mary Berry's monthly hairspray bill. How set is that woman's hair? She could bake a Genoese sponge while a troupe of Morris dancers rodgered her from behind and that hair would NOT move a millimetre.

Unfortunately, I didn't have the services of the very lovely Kirsty Allsop to hunt out the best buys in the area, so it was all down to me to decide what I wanted. I'm not sure how that poor woman keeps her cool dealing with the unrealistic lunatics with a £200K budget who'll accept nothing less than a five-bedroom townhouse in Henley-on-Thames with an unobscured view of the river and a kitchen the size of Luxembourg.

Although my expectations were a little more realistic, I did have a few things that were on my list of 'must haves' or 'nice to haves'. A small private garden would be nice. I'd really missed being able to sit out in the privacy of my own garden after a hard day's work. No more avoiding the neighbours for fear of being ogled or told about the 'Fucking idiot that needs his bollocks chopping off for not parking in the designated area'. A bit harsh as he was only there for about ten minutes and he did have a disabled sticker on his car.

Two bedrooms, which would mean I could accommodate drunken friends without having to vacate my nice comfy bed for the joys of sleeping in the lounge on a glorified lilo. I'd bought a good quality airbed but, at the end of the day you still only had to move an inch and you'd be rolling off it with the grace of an intoxicated rhino. More importantly than this though, having the extra bedroom would mean my son Adam could stay over, making my new house more like his home too.

Nor did I want a ramshackle old relic; the thought of buying a property that would involve enlisting the help of a builder with an arse crack the size of the Grand Canyon who drank more tea than China could produce in a year, was a challenge I could do without. My experiences of building folk have always been a bit hit-and-miss, the worst being when a particularly uncouth individual performed his daily ablutions at my house; I understand that we all have to go, but the vision of his impaled number two on the end of my designer toilet brush is one that would need months of therapy to erase from my memory.

Location Location Location, as the programme tells us, is *very* important. You don't want to end up living someplace where an ASBO is considered a qualification. A cursory drive around any neighbourhood will give you an indication of how nice it is based on how many BNP stickers are displayed in windows, and how many groups of feral youths you see congregated on the street corners dressed in hoodies drinking White Lightning and sniffing lighter fuel.

Off-road parking would be good. As I make Stevie Wonder look proficient at parallel parking; a driveway is a definite plus if I didn't want to spend half of my life driving around looking for a space near my house that was big enough to fit a Sherman Tank in.

Slightly thicker walls should also be a consideration. Having lived somewhere that had walls with the resonance of a damp piece of loo roll, this was a definite must.

NO FREAKING MAGGOTS. This surely should be on everybody's list but may not automatically spring to mind.

Ideally, I would love to have stayed in the Knutsford area. I know you may think that my description of the tap-dancing lunatic who swore like a Glaswegian docker makes the area seem like a magnet for the mentally unhinged, but actually it's a really nice place to live. But very expensive. As it would take the luck of an Irish leprechaun stood at the end of a rainbow with a horseshoe for me to afford something bigger than a shed in somebody's garden, I needed to cast my house-buying net a little further than the leafy suburbs of Cheshire.

Before completely ruling out the possibility of sharing my postcode with the twin-set and pearl brigade of the Cheshire Crochet Club, I did go to see a couple of properties. This was in the vain hope that one day, should I feel the urge to produce a nice lace doily to put my lamp on, I would have the expert tuition close at hand.

The first place, although a flat, was described as a good size and well decorated throughout. It was also on the ground floor with an 'enclosed space' at the back and a 'delightful little fenced patio area' at the front. It didn't tick all the boxes but you have to take a chance sometimes and go and see somewhere to really get a feel for it, you never know.

As I was keen to ensure that Adam liked any house that I'd potentially be living in, he came with me for the viewing. Although his house-buying skills were on a par with Mother Theresa's prowess in the bedroom, his opinion was crucial. Let's face it, it's always good to have another nosey bugger to look round somewhere so that you can swap observations later too.

With the help of Aida, we found the area where the flat was located, and immediately realised what an absolute pile of rocking horse excrement the spec of the property was! It was obvious that the charlatan of an estate agent had taken inspiration from Hans Christian Andersen. This could have been in a veiled attempt to woo some poor blind person to the property who wouldn't notice the location: it was slap bang in the middle of a row of shops. Hmmm...a slight oversight or and intended omission? Not only that but, as we parked up in front of the next door's café, we couldn't fail to notice that the enclosed delightful patio area was neither delightful nor enclosed. I had visons of waking up one morning to find somebody sitting there waiting for their skinny cappuccino to be delivered. What Mr Andersen had also failed to mention, in his oh-so-nonfactual advertisement, was that it was situated directly next to a busy road, and when I say next to, I mean next to. If you had a backside larger than your average size ten, you'd be at risk of getting at least one side of your arse shaved off by an unsuspecting motorist as you exited the property. As I was contemplating whether to even bother going in to look at the property Adam must have read my mind.

'Who the hell converts a shop into a flat and thinks that somebody would want to live there? You'd have to be have the common sense of a plank of wood to even look round it.' That's ma boy…say it how it is!!

You'll not be surprised to hear that we didn't even wait for the estate agent to turn up, instead opting to ring them to say that perhaps they needed to add a few more facts to their description so as not to waste people's time. Unless they can find a caffeine addict that enjoys bus spotting, I had a feeling that the place would be about as easy to sell as an open top jeep tour of Syria. Not a great start.

The next property in Knutsford was described as 'Needs a little modernisation'. This was once again stretching the truth to the levels of Kim Kardashian's knicker elastic. Instead of opting for the subtle glow of Apricot White, these colour-blind lunatics thought that by painting the walls the same shade as a bottle of Sunny Delight, they had created an ambiance of warmth and a welcoming summer glow. In reality, it gave me a tension headache within about five minutes of walking around. It wasn't just the décor that made this property about as appealing as a poke in the eye with a cattle prod, it was again the location. It seemed that for me to be able to afford anything in the Knutsford area, I'd have to live where nobody else wanted to. As a plus, the house did have ample parking and a nice little courtyard at the rear. Nevertheless, added to the hallucinogenic decorating, you would also have to contend with the glow of the flickering traffic lights that were situated just outside the window; it would be like living in sensory overload.

Having widened my search criteria to areas where I thought I could afford and would like to live, I then entered the world of enlightenment to just how some people live. The biggest shock when house viewing is that some people believe that tidying up and running the hoover round before a viewing isn't necessary in order to sell. Unbelievable, right? I went to a number of places where I thought I'd stumbled into a jumble sale with items of clothing, some destined for the washing basket, strewn around the place. It was no good then saying, 'Oh sorry. Excuse the mess,' as I walked away with a pair of dirty knickers stuck to the bottom of my shoe. All they had to do was shove it in a cupboard until I'd gone. Some people also believe that cleanliness is not next to godliness even when trying to sell your house. It's quite difficult to see the property's potential when the kitchen looks like a crumb bomb has exploded and the lounge carpet has more stains than your average nightclub.

Then there was another place I viewed that had a front door that transported you back in time. Having been met by a lady resembling Brian May and wearing a

Pippa Dee tied silk blouse styled on *Dynasty*, we then proceeded with a tour of the property in a cloud of Rive Gauche. My God. It was like I'd been transported back to my teenage years as I walked into one bedroom. Here I was faced with exactly the same pink and grey zig zag wallpaper that I'd had. Granted the posters of Paul Young and U2 were absent though. It did make me wonder if the house had been untouched since the decade that fashion forgot. The lounge sported a metal framed red sofa that looked about as relaxing as sitting in a hospital waiting area, and a black glass coffee table, that exposed enough fingerprints to have my Mum racing for her chamois leather. And the kitchen! That had a lowered ceiling with coloured plastic opaque panels and fluorescent tubes that shone through giving the impression you were in a dingy jazz club rather than somewhere to rustle up a black forest gateau. Never mind modernisation, it needed a complete overhaul to drag it kicking and screaming into this millennium.

The last place on my list turned out to be the darkest dankest property on earth, aside from Mr Bin Laden's cave dwelling residence. The house did have windows, but during the viewing the blinds remained completely drawn letting in about as much light as a trip down the Blue John Mines. It was like negotiating your way around a Hollister store, and trust me I've said, 'Oops sorry' to more pot plants than I care to remember in there. The impression of dinginess wasn't helped by the fact that most of the décor ranged from charcoal to chocolate. I thought I saw a clump of mushrooms in one corner, but as I would have needed night vision goggles to determine this, it could just as easily have been a rug. Unsurprisingly, the bloke showing me round had the same complexion as a bowl of cold porridge, and the unnerving way that he kept licking his lips made me wish the estate agent would hurry getting there. For a change, the part of my brain that was too polite to offend was overruled by the sensible segment that shouted, *'Get the hell out of here.'*

So, after a quick look at the downstairs with my finger firmly on my speed dial, I made my excuses to leave. I wasn't sure if the look of disappointment was due to not getting the sale, or missing the opportunity to pickle my body parts and store them in a large jar in the larder.

It seemed that finding a property that didn't need decontaminating or drastically re-decorating was virtually impossible. Damn it. I was just about to give up hope and renew my tenancy, when I stumbled across a small three bedroomed semi that, although a fraction more expensive, seemed ideal. I didn't know the area well, but it wasn't far from where I previously lived so I knew you didn't need steel bars on your windows and a direct dial to a security company to live there. I decided there was no harm in taking a peek as what's the worst that could happen? I see it and love it, then I have to camp out on their doorstep until they take pity on my poor frozen soul and drop the price slightly.

Despite the photos looking good, Adam and I now turned up with an element of scepticism that they were in any way a precise representation of reality. They usually turned out to be about as accurate as opinion polls. They may as well employ the services of Paul the Psychic Octopus to enlighten us for the good they do.

On this occasion, no stretching of the truth had taken place and as soon as I walked in I got a good feeling. You just know, don't you? The last house I'd bought had a pine-cladded lounge wall, a maroon bathroom suite with matching tiles, and a kitchen that had been fitted before the Second World War…. but we loved the feel of it.

The amiable lady who owned this house was very informative telling us all about the property, the history and the neighbours. No dodgy perverts or swearing banshees, just nice families. It all looked newly decorated with good sized rooms, a great fitted kitchen and even a downstairs loo. The cherry on top was the private, attractive south-facing garden that was completely enclosed. Perfect for Ferdinand. It ticked all my boxes, Adam loved it, and not a single maggot in sight.

Typical. The right house but just above the right price. Oh well, nothing ventured nothing gained. So, with a mixture of trepidation and excitement, I rang the very next day to put an offer in. I was more on edge than a junkie at a methadone clinic as I waited for their response. As my nails were about to be shredded for the second time, they came back …. It was a yes. They'd accepted it!

I couldn't believe my luck that I'd managed to get such a bargain. Normally I'm absolutely useless at these things. I even ended up paying over the odds for a tablecloth I didn't want when I went to a medina in Tunisia. Only a twerp with the bartering abilities of a naive idiot would pay full price for something that they not only didn't need, but actually didn't like. Pity had come into my inadequate negotiations skills. The canny stallholder obviously saw me as a soft touch, putting on a BAFTA winning performance of a penniless old lady with arthritic hands who'd spent hours of painful labour creating the massive doily for the table. I fell for it hook, line, and sinker.

Fortunately, I was not dealing with an unscrupulous Tunisian market trader this time, and the couple were just as keen to get things moving quickly as they'd put in an offer on a house that they truly loved and, as I had no chain, I was perfect for them too.

The weeks that followed saw my stress levels rise from mildly irritated to hit the bloody roof annoyed as my incompetent solicitors took longer than a learner driver to get in gear. I even made a trip into Manchester city centre to deliver signed papers to their head office on a night that saw rain levels on a par with an African monsoon.

It was a good job I was in constant touch with the vendor, she kicked ass better than Uma Thurman with

PMT, although ever so slightly less violently.

Once I knew that everything was on track, I rang my landlord to give notice on the house of horrors. It was a good job I'd left it until then, as the following day he'd had it photographed and advertised; it then rented quicker than a beach hut in Brighton. Obviously, a sought-after area and an ideal starter home for the young couple trying out life together. I didn't tell them about the flesh-eating occupants or the walls made out of rice paper. I also left out specifics relating to the colourful neighbours. It's better that people make their own judgement and find out for themselves. Like I had.

23

New Pad and New Beginning

How the hell had I managed to amass so much crap in such a short space of time? In a house the size of an elephant's shoe box, I had somehow succeeded to still fill a stack of big boxes with my junk. I know that junk is not the most eloquent way of conveying my life's possessions, but it's the most suitable way to describe the mish-mash of items that were now being expertly wrapped and packaged ready for transportation to my new home.

An element of chucking away and charity giveaways had taken place; I'm not one of these people who keeps an old pair of slippers just in case the new ones fall apart quicker than some contestants on *Britain's Got Talent*. Saying that though, I still kept hold of some clothes that I'm sure will never be worn again, including a fluffy white muff, a lime green dress and a lovely pair of orange shoes... Well you never know... I could be invited to a fancy dress ball for the colour blind and clinically insane. By the way, if you're ever looking to buy a muff, never ever google 'cheap muffs'. The results will make your eyes water and you'll undoubtedly be on somebody's watch list somewhere!

My friends Laura and Gill were helping me on the morning of the move. My sister Katy, nephew Daniel and Adam were then all arriving later in the day armed with marigolds and muscles. As the majority of my belongings were boxed, and I didn't have a lot of furniture, I'd decided to hire a van rather than pay a removal company. What I didn't factor in was the dismantling and moving of the bed. This had been assembled in situ upstairs, but now needed to come apart in order to bring it down the narrow stairway.

What a palaver! We first of all tried just taking one end off in the hope it would then fit. Nope. Still too big. We then took the headboard end off. Buggery bugger, it still didn't fit. Next to come off was one side. Shit, no good. Finally, the last side was removed which just left the frame with all the slats still in place…until we moved it downstairs. It looked like a skeleton of a Minke whale lay strewn on the stairway by the time we'd manoeuvred it unsuccessfully around the corner. Fortunately, the wall and paintwork had not taken much of a bashing, unlike my arms which looked like I'd been in a cat fight with a particularly vicious tabby. Still, we'd managed to get it down with all the screws and bolts safely boxed away…even if it was now in 50 pieces and would take somebody with a degree in bed engineering to put it back together.

As I'd never driven a van before, I'd opted to hire one that was a transit size, so although I didn't have that much to transport, it would still take a few trips once I'd got the keys to Casa Isobel. I confess to being a bit apprehensive when I'd gone to pick the van up the day before the move. I consider myself to be a good driver, despite having the parking abilities of a short-sighted penguin, but the prospect of having to manoeuvre a vehicle larger than anything I'd ever driven before was a bit different. But my God… I turned into the White Van Woman instantly…I loved it!

I'm not saying that I thought I owned the road and started to cut people up and drove like a complete tosser, but they are deceptively easy to drive and do give you a feeling of superiority as you look down on the minions in their small insignificant vehicles. Not only that but, who'd have thought it, I actually found it easier to park; unless I just didn't actually see what I was hitting!

With the first van loaded and the rented place cleaned, it was then time to anxiously await the call to say everything had gone through and I could finally go to the estate agents to get the keys.

I was giddier than a giddy kipper from Giddyminster. It took forever!!

By two o'clock I'd just about bitten all my newly grown nails back to the bone in apprehension. Laura was worried that I was then going to start gnawing on her digits too, so told me in no uncertain terms to just bloody ring the woman I was buying off to see if she knew what the delay was. For goodness sake! It turned out she'd dropped the keys off at her estate agent a couple of hours ago at the agreed time!

Although relieved that there had been no last-minute hiccups, and the house was now mine (Eeek), I was still a bit miffed at the estate agents who should've called to say the keys were there; that was two hours and ten fingernails wasted. Things didn't improve any when I got there either, as the trainee bullshitter swore blind that he didn't have them! This however, was swiftly rectified when I got 'Uma' on the phone. I almost felt sorry for the poor lad as he visibly shrunk with every sharp word delivered into his lughole. The keys it seemed had been filed against the wrong property. Aaargghhhh!

Fortunately, as they were on an easily identifiable key ring of a fluffy ball that had seen better days, they were simple to locate once the misunderstanding had been identified. It was with a multitude of apologies and a noticeably quivering hand that the now nervous estate agent handed over what looked like a set of keys attached to hairy bollock.

Wahoooooooooooo…I was now smiling from ear to ear like I'd won the lottery. I'd actually bought my very own house. I couldn't believe it.

I was so eager to see it that I just couldn't wait to get there. White Van Woman now inhabited my inner soul as I drove the short distance to the house as quickly as I could with Laura following close behind.

Miracle of miracles, I even managed to reverse onto the drive, perhaps at the cost of a small patch of grass, but without any structural damage to my new house….MY NEW HOUSE… I was so excited!!

You know when you have a viewing and you think that you take everything in? Well, let me tell you that you don't. Don't get me wrong, the house was still absolutely perfect and if anything without the furniture it looked even better. But how the hell had I missed the most bizarre light fittings that you are ever likely to see outside of the Tate Modern? It's not like I'd have needed to look up much to see the one in the lounge! Without the coffee table that had been there previously, you practically walked into what can only be described as a huge chandelier cascading in all its glittery magnificence from the ceiling. At the other end, in the dining room, was another one which could feasibly be doubled up as a table centre piece. Even my head tinkled them as I walked under, so for anybody of average height, it could conceivably end up with a trip to the eye hospital were they not careful. Laura's reaction said it all…

'Good Lord. They're big!'

And these weren't the only unique light fittings to adorn the ceilings. One of my favourites was the one in the downstairs lavatory. Or as we affectionately named it The Dolphin Room. The reason being the large blue plastic dolphin that was dangling above the toilet giving the impression that it had leaped from the bowl in an attempt to perform a double back flip. Bizarre to say the least. I could see I needed an urgent appointment at the local opticians to check if I was suffering from 'light fitting blindness', which apparently had also been passed on genetically to my son.

Venturing upstairs, the light in the master bedroom would have been better in a Moroccan brothel than a three-bed semi on a housing estate in Manchester. And the reason for this assessment? Well it possibly had something to do with the fact that the holes where the light shone through were shaped like an erect cock and balls! This meant that each morning I could wake up, stare up at the ceiling and think, 'Bollocks'. A normal reaction to the alarm sounding most days, mind you.

The two other bedrooms were not as phallic with a row of spotlights on a metal frame, but again these were slightly oversized for the rooms giving the impression you were either about to have your spleen removed in an operating theatre or you were being taken for interrogation for crimes against the country. These people liked their rooms bright! It certainly made the house tours interesting with people's comments raging from ….

'What the fuck?'…not my Mum obviously.

'Erm. Did you know you've got illuminated genitals on your ceiling?' …Again, not my Mum.

'I just paid a visit with Flipper dangling on my head'… Clearly a man.

'Oh my word that's horrendous, and look at the

dust on it'...Yep, you've guessed it! That was my Mum.

After the initial inspection, smiling like an idiot, it was time to get down to the business of moving the rest of my gear. You'll be surprised to hear that this actually went really smoothly with no breakages and no accidents. This could have been down to Laura's epic organisational and loading skills rather than good luck though. I'm sure that woman could herd a colony of feral cats and still have time to file her tax returns.

As I left the rented house for the last time, I took a reflective look around. My stay here had certainly had its ups and downs, but it had allowed me the time I needed to decide what I really wanted to do. It had also given me the confidence to be on my own and enjoy my own space, whilst realising that there was a new life for me if I wanted it. Granted, along with all this it had also given me sleepless nights, had put me off egg fried rice for the foreseeable future and confirmed that I am a bit of a buffoon who shouldn't be trusted around wheelie bins.

By the time I got back to my new house, the rest of my trusted helpers had arrived and had a good old nosey around. Adam and Daniel were given the unenviable task of putting the Minke Whale back together so it resembled a wooden bed. Katy sorted out the kitchen, ergonomically putting everything in the correct location for ease of use (she's always been a clever bugger), whilst Laura, Gill and I cleaned and unboxed the rest of my knick-knacks.

By the time my Mum and Dad arrived with Ferdinand in the evening we were pretty much sorted. Although, as the furniture I owned was so sparse, you could have been forgiven for thinking that half the load had been lost in transit.

As Ferdinand raced through the door, skidding unceremoniously on the unfamiliar wooden floor, he was off snuffling his way around every nook and cranny like a sniffer dog going cold turkey. Where his nose didn't fit he shoved it anyway. There had been cats in the house previously so he was on the hunt to locate and destroy. He seemed to like it though, especially the garden; I could see I was going to have problems getting him to stay in!

I looked around at all my family and friends gathered here in my new home as I was about to start the next leg of my journey. I'll always look back on my life before now with extreme fondness and I'll have a special place in my heart for everybody who's been part of it; especially my ex-husband who I will always love for giving me the most precious thing in my life in Adam. But now the time was right for us both to move on.

I'd come such a long way since taking the brave decision to do something about being unhappy. I was proud that I'd not just accepted how things were, but actually got off my wobbly backside and done something about it. Sometimes the easiest thing is to just moan and whinge that things aren't good. But I'd actually grabbed the bloody great big bull by his horns to give my life a much needed shake. I'd gone completely out of my comfort zone to try new things in an attempt to make the most of my life.

I know it's a cliché, but life really is too short so why settle for being unhappy and making all those around you unhappy when you can make a complete tit of yourself and provide those around you with a laugh instead. Happiness and misery are both infectious, so in my book it's always better to spread a bit of joy and grasp what life has to offer.

I didn't know how things would pan out with Peter, I don't necessarily see him as Mr Right, but he's certainly Mr Right Now. Although who knows, the gods do enjoy sending you the odd curve ball now and then to keep you on your toes. All I knew was what I had at the moment was fun and just what the doctor ordered, and it gave Duracell a chance to replenish their diminished stock. I'd been sure to pack Vernon away somewhere nice and safe, the last thing I needed was Ferdinand to unearth him from a bag of knickers and think he was one of his toy bones.

The most important things I have in my life are my great family and wonderful friends. They've got me through some tough times, and for that I'll be eternally grateful. Sometimes their advice hasn't always been the best, a case in point being when Gill said,

'Don't worry that shampoo for blondes may look purple but it just makes your hair brighter'. Does it bollocks. I walked around for at least a week looking like I'd gone 'old lady blue' before the bugger finally faded!

I wished that Em could have been here with me on this special day to share the moment. Although to be fair if she had been then I'm sure the first thing to be unpacked would have been the corkscrew and then it would have been all downhill after that. No ergonomically designed kitchen more like an inebriated designed one.

Talking of which, it was time to crack open the champagne; corks were popped and glasses filled ready to toast my new start in my new home. Even Ferdinand got in on the act barking incessantly at what he perceived to be his feline mortal enemy strolling through the garden.

I absolutely adored my new house, even the light fittings were a feature. I had such a great feeling about it and just knew that I would be happy here surrounded by all the people I loved.

Just as we were about to raise our glasses my phone rang. A number from the other side of the world.

A perfect end to the day. And a perfect new start…

About the Author

Lorraine Hopkins, fast approaching her half century milestone, thought it high time she wrote her first book. Living in Manchester and weekending in the Lake District she combines a witty outlook with a lust for life and, for good measure, a dose of keen observational skills.

Hilarious and comical, often at her own expense, this is sure to be the first of many as she pens her high jinks and jaunts in her own inimitable way.

You can contact Lorraine at lhopkins.author@gmail.com

You can follow her on Twitter: @Loz_F_Factor